NIGHT OF THE
SHIFTER'S MOON

Read all the Unicorns of Balinor books:

#1 The Road to Balinor
#2 Sunchaser's Quest
#3 Valley of Fear
#4 By Fire, By Moonlight
#5 Search for the Star
#6 Secrets of the Scepter
#7 Night of the Shifter's Moon

Coming soon . . .

#8 Shadows over Balinor

UNICORNS OF BALINOR

NIGHT OF THE SHIFTER'S MOON

MARY STANTON

AN
APPLE
PAPERBACK

SCHOLASTIC INC.
New York Toronto London Auckland Sydney
Mexico City New Delhi Hong Kong

No part of this publication may be reproduced, stored in a retrieval system, or transmitted in any form or by any means, electronic, mechanical, photocopying, recording, or otherwise, without written permission of the publisher. For information regarding permission, write to Scholastic Inc., Attention: Permissions Department, 555 Broadway, New York, NY 10012.

ISBN 0-439-16786-8

12 11 10 9 8 7 6 5 4 3 2 1   0 1 2 3 4 5/0

Printed in the U.S.A.   40
First Scholastic printing, March 2000

For Jim Goff

NIGHT OF THE
SHIFTER'S MOON

1

Rain fell on the Forest of Ardit and silvered the tops of the logan trees. There was one road through Ardit, and it was filled with puddles. A pair of rabbits splashed across the road. Sheltering under a gooseberry bush, they began to groom themselves dry. Suddenly, a magnificent cream-and-mahogany collie ran by. Both rabbits sat bolt upright in alarm, ears quivering.

"Is that a dog?!" the rabbit Bayberry demanded indignantly. "A dog! A dog?! His Majesty ought to *ban* dogs from the forest! And the next time I see His Majesty, I shall tell him so, right to his face!"

"Hold on!" Bayberry's companion, Snowdrop, peeked out from the bush and stared down the road. A group of travelers followed the dog. Three unicorns and three riders. Was it . . . no! It couldn't be! His pink nose twitched in amazement. Snowdrop turned his head to Bayberry and whispered urgently, "You'd tell His Majesty, Lord of the Animals in Balinor — the Sunchaser himself — to ban dogs from the Forest of Ardit?"

Bayberry nodded smugly. "I would."

"And the Princess Arianna? You'd tell her — right to her face? You wouldn't be scared or anything?"

Bayberry stuck out his chest and puffed out his cheeks. Despite rumors of their return, *he* knew that the Princess and the Sunchaser had been gone from Balinor for a long time, hiding from the evil Shifter. So he felt perfectly safe in saying, "Why, you bet I would!" He stroked his whiskers with his front paws in a very self-important way. "Why, just put me in front of His Majesty and Her Royal Highness and watch me tell them a thing or two! All I need is a chance!"

Snowdrop crept back under the bush. In a few seconds, the travelers would pass by the gooseberry bush where the rabbits were hidden. "Well, Bayberry, you big boastful rabbit! You've got your chance!" Quick as a wink, Snowdrop whirled and kicked poor Bayberry onto the road. He tumbled into a puddle. A young girl's voice called, "Halt!" There was the jangling of harnesses, the stamp of unicorn hooves, and then a second girl's voice said crossly, "It's just a silly rabbit!"

Bayberry picked himself up, full of indignation. Three unicorns stood in the middle of the road, each with a rider. Bayberry twitched the rain out of

2

his ears and started to scold the bronze-haired girl on the tall bronze unicorn. "If," he began, "you humans would just watch where . . ." His eyes grew wide as he recognized the girl and the unicorn before him. His jaw dropped, and he stuttered, "Ah, ah — Your Royal Highness! Your Majesty!" And he sank into a huddled bow.

"Go ahead!" Snowdrop giggled from the safety of the gooseberry bush. "Tell the Sunchaser all about getting rid of dogs in the forest!"

"You don't want dogs in the forest?" a voice said in his ear. Bayberry jumped three feet into the air. The big collie had returned from scouting the road ahead. Goodness, his teeth were sharp! Bayberry squeaked and shut his eyes tight.

"Now, Lincoln! You've scared the poor little thing!" Her Royal Highness, Princess Arianna, bent down from the saddle and smoothed the collie's ears. "Rabbit, I'm so sorry we almost ran over you."

"Make . . . make . . . make nothing of it, Your Highness!" Bayberry said in a sheepish voice. His nose twitched with joy. "But you are back in Balinor, Princess! And His Majesty!" He looked shyly at his liege lord. The great unicorn's long mane was damp with rain, and his ebony horn dripped pearly drops of water. But he glowed with the special bronze fire of his rank: the Sunchaser, Lord of the Animals in Balinor. "We never thought we'd see you again!"

"We have been back for some time," Ari told the rabbit. "But up until now we have had to keep our whereabouts a secret. Who knows where the Shifter's spies are these days! Now, my friend," she added in a kindly way, "can you tell me your name?"

"Bayberry, milady," the rabbit said humbly.

"Pssst!" Snowdrop whispered from the bush. "What about me?"

"And my friend there. His name is Snow-drop."

Snowdrop crept out of the bushes, wriggling with delight.

"Well, Bayberry, Snowdrop. You have met my collie, Lincoln. And this is Finn, captain of the Royal cavalry."

Finn nodded hello. Privately, Bayberry thought the boy didn't look much like a captain of the cavalry. He was thin, with hazel-colored eyes. Freckles were sprinkled on his face and he had a lot of red hair that the rain had made very curly. But Finn was riding a wonderful unicorn! What a glorious beast! He was almost as tall as the Sunchaser. And the glorious red ruby jewel at the base of his horn meant he was one of the Royal unicorns, at least. Bayberry knew that only Royal unicorns and Celestial unicorns possessed a precious jewel at the base of their horns, which held the unicorn's own personal magic.

"Finn is riding Rednal," Ari continued. "And this is Lori Carmichael. She rides Tobiano." She smiled at the second girl. "That is, she's riding Toby

4

now. Up until yesterday she rode a unicorn named Stalwart."

"Hi," Lori Carmichael said. She had blond hair pulled back in a ponytail. Bayberry recognized the voice that had called him a silly rabbit.

"I'll bet Stalwart bucked her off!" Bayberry muttered to himself.

"That's what *you* think!" the blond girl said rudely. "I left Stalwart with Ari's old nurse to give her a hand. And Finn brought me Tobiano to ride!" Tobiano was short and stout, although the black diamond at the base of his horn meant he was a Royal unicorn, too, if not something even more marvelous.

"Perhaps you can help us, Bayberry," the Princess said, her voice kind. "We are looking for a lake. We have just come from a visit to my old nurse, Dr. Bohnes, and she said that we had to make a stop at the lake and spend the night, before we proceed home to Balinor. It is called the Lake of the Path to the Moon. Do you know it?"

"I know it," Snowdrop said loudly. He had hopped out onto the road and sat on his haunches gazing worshipfully at Ari and Chase, oblivious to the rain. "Ask me! Ask me!"

"I know the way better than you do," Bayberry hissed at him. "Hush. She asked *me*!"

"Her Royal Highness requires an answer," the Sunchaser said. And his voice was so deep and so majestic that both rabbits fell into giggling confusion and couldn't say anything at all.

Ari ran her hand down Chase's neck and said, "Now, Chase. You've scared them!"

Bayberry, who had squeezed his eyes shut, opened one and looked at his Princess. There was a smile on her face, and her sapphire-blue eyes were alight with laughter. "Go straight down the road," he squeaked. "Then turn left at the three-branched tree."

"Thank you," the Princess said. "We must go, Bayberry. Good-bye, and thank you. Good-bye, Snowdrop."

And with that, the Royal party went off down the road to search for the Lake of the Path to the Moon. Snowdrop and Bayberry hopped back excitedly to their warren, where none of the other rabbits believed for two seconds that they had met the Sunchaser himself.

Ari and Chase continued on their damp and weary way. It had been two days since Finn had met them with Rednal and Toby, and three days since Ari had visited her old nurse, Dr. Bohnes. She had gotten the certification required by the Lords of Balinor to show that she was indeed the Princess of Balinor. *We could have saved ourselves a trip*, she thought at Chase. *All Puckenstew, Artos, and Rexel had to do was ask those rabbits. They knew us without any certificate!*

6

Chase, his eyes alert for the tree with three branches ahead, merely whickered in reply.

They rode on in damp and drippy silence. Lori shifted restlessly on the sturdy black-and-white unicorn, Tobiano. "I'm wet!" Lori said crossly.

Nobody said anything to this.

"And I'm hungry!"

Tobiano flicked one ear back and muttered something under his breath. He splashed through a large puddle and a big splotch of mud landed on Lori's boot. Lori drew up hard on the reins. Toby planted all four hooves in the mud and stopped cold. "Quit that!" he said.

"You started it!"

Finn turned around in the saddle and gave Lori a reproving look. It was very bad manners to pull at a unicorn's mouth. Ahead of him, Ari recognized the signs of a quarrel. She shifted her weight slightly backward, and Chase halted obediently. She tapped his flank lightly with one booted heel and flexed her right rein. Chase turned around at this command so that he and his mistress faced the others. "It's only a few miles to the lake," Chase said. Rain dripped from his coal-black horn and plastered his silky mane against his neck. "And all of us are wet, Lori."

"You're not as wet as I am," Lori grumbled. "I'm squishing in the saddle! You've got all that magic now, Ari. Can't you use some of it to get the sun to come out?"

Ari couldn't help but smile. She did have all the magic, or at least all the magic she was supposed to have. The quest to retrieve the trio of gold rings belonging to the Royal Scepter had been successful. And now with the Scepter fully charged with magic, she and her friends would be on their way home to Balinor after a night spent on the Lake of the Path to the Moon. Ari and Chase were ready for their greatest task: to overthrow the evil Shifter and return her to the throne. "I don't think I can do anything about the sun, can I, Chase?"

"I doubt it, milady. But you can always ask." His deep voice was amused.

"The Royal Scepter hasn't said a word since the trio of gold rings was recovered," Ari said. "I suppose I could try again."

"Go ahead and ask, then," Lori said crossly. "I'm getting mold all over me. It hasn't stopped raining since we started this stupid trip!"

"The Scepter will not speak until it is time," Chase said.

"It doesn't matter, we need the rain," Finn said. "It's good for the land. Back home in Deridia, we used to pray to the Dreamspeaker for rain. Honestly, Lori, you don't want Her Royal Highness . . ."

"Finn!" Ari said. "You promised not to 'Royal Highness' me anymore!"

"I mean, Ari," Finn said shyly. The red-haired boy had come from the desert country of Deridia, where he had worked in his parents' Inn. He still wasn't all that comfortable around royalty, even though he and Ari had been through many adventures together. "Anyhow, no human — or unicorn for that matter — should mess around with nature."

"Why not?" Lori demanded.

Finn floundered a bit at this. "Well, I . . ."

"The rising and the setting of the sun, the movements of the moon, the flow of the tides, all these are part of the Deep Magic," Tobiano grumbled. "Any fool knows that. And any fool knows that no human or animal this side of the Celestial Valley should fool with the Deep Magic." He stamped his hooves in the puddle again. Mud flew up, and Lori shrieked.

Rednal — who spoke little but observed a great deal — said, "Perhaps we ought to make a fire and dry out a bit, Finn. Rain doesn't bother us unicorns at all — as a matter of fact, we rather enjoy it. But I can tell that you're uncomfortable. And my withers itch under the saddle."

Finn looked a question at Ari.

"I suppose we could make a fire and dry out a bit," she said. "What do you think, Chase?"

The huge bronze unicorn didn't answer. He stood with his neck arched, ears up, dark eyes fixed on a dense grove of trees on the south side of the road. Then he said, "The rabbit Bayberry said to turn left at the tree with the three branches!"

"Yes. Do you see it, Chase?"

He shook himself. "It's right over there. But

beyond it, in the dark of the woods . . . I heard something."

Startled, Ari rose a little in her stirrups, then settled into the saddle again. "What did you hear? The Shifter's soldiers?"

Chase was silent. Every muscle in his great body tensed.

"What did you hear?" Ari asked again.

"I heard it, too," Rednal said softly.

"Me too," Toby said with a gruff snort. "I thought I heard . . ."

"Atalanta," Rednal said in that same soft voice.

Atalanta! The Dreamspeaker! The Twilight Mare was mate of Numinor, the Golden One, ruler of the Celestial Valley!

"I hear the bells of her harness," Chase said. "She calls."

The unicorns looked at one another. Suddenly, Ari was forcibly reminded that all three — Rednal, Toby, and Chase himself — were kin to one another.

There were four kinds of unicorns in Balinor and the lands beyond it: those who lived and worked with the people, called Worker unicorns; the Royal unicorns, who served the Royal House of Balinor; and the Celestial unicorns, those magical beings from the Celestial Valley. There was also a fourth breed, seldom seen by humans. They were the Wild Ones. Ari had met one, and privately thought that they were a mixture of runaway Royals and Workers.

In peaceful times, the only Celestial unicorn to walk the land of the humans was the Sunchaser, Lord of the Animals. Bonded to the Princess of the Royal House of Balinor, the Lord of the Animals was the link between animals and humans that allowed all beings in Balinor to talk with one another.

But these were not peaceful times.

"What's going on with you guys?" Lori asked Toby rudely. Finn shook his head in exasperation. Lori was not from Balinor — she had found her way accidentally to Balinor from Glacier River Farm, beyond the Gap — and Finn had always thought her selfish rudeness was because she was a foreigner.

Ari knew better. Lori was, well — Lori.

"What shall we do, Chase?" Ari asked. She strained her ears, but she couldn't hear the crystal chime of bells that told her that the Dreamspeaker was near. She couldn't hear anything at all but the steady rain.

"Walk on," Rednal said. "Dr. Bohnes told us to go to the lake. There is the tree with the three branches. The way is marked."

"But Dr. Bohnes didn't say anything about the Dreamspeaker," Toby said.

"If she calls, we must go," Ari said firmly. "And she calls us to the lake. So that is where we turn."

"I want to get DRY!" Lori complained loudly. "I don't care where we go!"

"Hush," Ari said. "Lead the way, Chase."

Finn, his hazel eyes bright with excitement,

11

threw back his hood and grasped his sword firmly in his right hand. "Do we head toward magic?" he asked eagerly.

"Even if we do," Ari said, "you won't need your sword." She loosened the reins and rode on the buckle. Chase stepped off the road and into the woods. He moved slowly, but with great assurance. Rednal and Toby fell into line behind him. Lincoln trotted at Chase's heels.

They were quickly swallowed up in the darkness of the trees and the thick brush. At first, Ari was alert, her eyes searching into the dimness of the forest, her ears straining for the magically sweet call of the Dreamspeaker.

Time passed. Ari didn't know how much or how little, which meant that they *were* headed toward magic. Her world contracted to the gentle fall of the rain, the pine scent of the forest, the soft whisper of the unicorns' hooves on the forest floor.

The day darkened. Night was near. At twilight, they broke through a thicket of trees to the banks of a mighty lake.

"The Lake of the Path to the Moon!" Toby said.

2

The Lake of the Path to the Moon was quiet and lovely. In the distance, gentle hills cupped the vast expanse of water. The shore was made entirely of small round pebbles that rolled back and forth with the gentle slap of the waves. In the lavender distance, the moon sailed behind a veil of rain.

Chase broke the silence. "Here," he said.

Ari slipped off his back and stumbled slightly when she hit the ground. She'd been in the saddle all day, and her knees and calves ached. She drew off her cloak and smoothed her hair. She stood at the shore of the lake in her long skirt and riding boots. Finn and Lori dismounted, too.

"Now what?" Lori demanded into the silence. "I want to build a fire! I want to eat!"

"Arianna and I must leave you for a while," Chase said gravely. "Finn, set about building a fire."

"You can't just leave us here!" Lori shrieked.

13

"That's enough!" Toby said. "I'd like a fire myself. Lincoln and I will go get some wood."

Ari faced the lake, knowing that she must leave her companions behind.

You must use the Scepter, milady, Chase said to Ari's mind. Ari glanced at him. *The Dreamspeaker wishes it.*

"All right," Ari whispered. Dr. Bohnes had told her strictly *not* to use the Scepter until the Dreamspeaker Atalanta had spoken to her. But Chase must be right. Chase was always right!

She drew the Royal Scepter from beneath her cloak. She held it up. The Scepter was made of carved rosewood, inlaid with lapis lazuli. A carved unicorn head with jeweled blue eyes was at the top. At the bottom of the shaft glowed the trio of gold rings. She had much to learn about the Royal magic; her mother, the Queen, had told her long ago that it would take time. But now she said — not knowing exactly where the words came from, but knowing they were right — "The rosewood shaft greets the crystal horn."

A crystal bell chimed in answer.

Ari said, "The child of the land greets the mother of the sky."

The Royal Scepter glowed like a rose. The moon floated out from behind the gauzy clouds and flooded the lake with brilliant light. The moonlight glimmered on the water, solidified, and made a crystal path. The chiming bells grew louder. Chase

14

buried his muzzle in Ari's hair and breathed out. *We must go.*

Wondering, Ari put one booted foot on the shining path to the moon. The crystal surface held. She took another step, then another. Chase walked gravely at her side. His mane flowed over his withers to his knees. His tail floated behind him. Ari's hair stirred in the breeze as they walked higher, ever higher, above the lake, seemingly to the face of the moon itself.

In the middle of the shining moonlight and at the end of the bridge, Ari could see the tall Crystal Arch, and beyond it, the gleam of velvety green grass. The scent of flowers came to her, and a soft breeze touched her cheek. The entrance to the arch glowed more brightly still. A unicorn stood there, her coat all the colors of lavender and violet. Her mane and tail were creamy white, and her elegant horn was crystal.

Ari looked down. Below her, the lake moved placidly in the moonlight. She could see the faces of her friends, openmouthed, gazing up at the great arch.

Ari looked up. Atalanta stood at the arch, her neck curved proudly, her great violet eyes glowing. Ari raised the Scepter in greeting. "Dreamspeaker!" she called.

"Welcome!" Atalanta nodded to them, then stepped aside.

Ari and Chase entered the Celestial Valley.

Ari stood at the top of the Crystal Arch and looked down into the Celestial Valley. The arch was a giant bridge, with one foot at the lakeshore, the crest at the entrance to the valley. The other foot led to the velvety green meadows of Atalanta's home. If she and Chase walked down this side of the arch, she would actually set foot in this fabled place.

"Welcome home, Sunchaser," Atalanta said. Golden sunlight flooded the valley, but Atalanta's violet glow was brighter than the sun itself. Her long, creamy eyelashes made her purple eyes look like violets surrounded by snowy leaves. A splendid veil of crimson velvet lay across her back and trailed down her flanks. The veil was embroidered with fantastical designs in silver: roses, crowns, peacocks, suns, and moons all entwined.

Ari was dazed. Her heart was full. She didn't know where to look first. To steady herself, she placed one hand on Chase's flank.

"It is good to be home again, Dreamspeaker," Chase said. He extended one foreleg and bowed to Atalanta, his black horn just touching the surface of the arch.

Atalanta bowed in return. "And welcome, Your Royal Highness, Arianna, Defender of the Bond, Daughter of Royals. The Rainbow herd greets you." Atalanta stepped aside, crimson veil swirling, to reveal more of the land beyond the arch. Ari gasped. The Celestial unicorns were assembled into the rainbow, beneath the bridge. The brilliant colors glowed with happy fire: reds shading to orange; orange mellowing to yellow; yellow to gold, green, blue, and indigo. Each Celestial unicorn held its head high and the magical jewel at the base of each horn combined to make a fireworks burst of color. Ari closed her eyes, dazzled.

Atalanta's voice was sweet and low. "Walk on, Princess, and meet the Celestial ones."

Ari straightened her back and held her head high. She hoped desperately that her knees wouldn't give way. *You don't look nervous,* Chase's deep voice assured her in her mind. *You look every inch a Princess.*

In these clothes? Ari responded. *I look like a bedraggled mess!*

They will not care, Chase again assured her.

Atalanta's eyes crinkled with amusement. She had caught Ari's thoughts! She tossed her head, and the crimson veil floated high over her flanks, then settled gracefully around Ari's shoulders. Ari gasped and smoothed the exquisite cloth with her hands.

You look royal, indeed, milady! Chase said.

"Thank you," Ari whispered aloud. "Thank you, Dreamspeaker."

She and Chase followed Atalanta down the walkway. With each step, more of the Celestial Valley was revealed to Ari's wondering eyes. The grass was thick, short, and dark green. Starflowers dotted the meadow. A deep river curved its turquoise way

17

through the grazing lands. Trees laden with golden leaves swayed on the riverbanks. A glitter of amethyst in the soft swell of hills on the other side of the river caught her eye.

The Watching Pool, Chase said in her mind. *We may see it yet, if the Twilight Mare agrees.*

The Twilight Mare! One of the many names of Atalanta! Ari wanted to pinch herself. She was here! She was really *here!*

Ari never remembered how she and Chase came to the end of the arch and set foot in the Celestial Valley for the very first time. She was too busy filling her heart and mind with the visions before her. The air was scented with the smell of flowers she had only dreamed of. The breeze was softer than any she had ever known before. And the sounds — the high sweet voices of the unicorn foals who played by the Imperial River, the singing of two mares in a happy duet, the bell-like splash of the water! The sounds were like nothing she had heard before.

Ari found herself on the granite path that led around the base of the arch to the Rainbow herd. She and Chase followed Atalanta to a spot facing the center of the row of unicorns. From here, she could see the entire Rainbow, end to end. Exactly in the middle was a huge unicorn, taller than the rest by two hands or more. He seemed to be made entirely of gold light: horn, hooves, and his whole magnificently muscled body.

"Numinor," Atalanta said, and Ari couldn't tell if the word was a command or a request. The great gold animal took a step forward and inclined his mighty neck.

"Your Highness!" Numinor said, his voice like thunder.

"Sir," Ari said shyly.

Numinor stepped back in line. Atalanta nodded, satisfied. She turned to Ari and lowered her head so that only Ari and Chase could hear her. "We have called you, Arianna, so that we may begin the Celestial Ceremony of Bonding. You have the Scepter."

It wasn't a question, but Ari nodded anyway. She held the Scepter up.

"Ah!" Atalanta sighed happily. "And the trio of gold rings completes it! We are ready to invest you with the Royal magic, Arianna. This was last done when your Royal mother was the eldest Princess of the House of Balinor. She and her unicorn had been bonded below, in the ceremony you and the Sunchaser celebrated before you were sent through the Gap. The Celestial Bonding is different. In the past, it was always done right after the ceremony in Balinor. And it would have been done for you and the Sunchaser — but the Shifter interfered and almost destroyed all. We have been waiting for this!"

"My mother was here before me?" Ari whispered. "She came to the Celestial Valley?"

"And her mother, too."

"She never spoke of it," Ari said.

"And you will not speak of it, either. This visit is only granted once in a lifetime. Hold the Scepter before you, my child."

Ari raised the Scepter high.

Then Atalanta spoke, her voice soft but clear, so that the words carried to every part of the valley. "Her Royal Highness has come again!"

"May the bond never break!" the Rainbow herd replied.

"The Royal magic is complete!" Atalanta cried with joy.

And the chorus responded again, "May the bond never break!"

"As enduring as earth!" Atalanta pawed once at the ground. Her hoof was made of the same crystal as her horn. The Rainbow herd stamped their hooves in response and the ground trembled with their force. Then Atalanta raised her head. Her horn sparkled and seemed to catch the sunlight. "As constant as the sun!" she cried.

Chase looked at Ari, his eyes deep and wise. Ari raised the Scepter higher, then twined her fingers in his mane. And Ari found herself shouting with them all, "May the bond never break!"

And then the unicorns sang. It was a song of hope, of love, of the ties that true friends have for one another. And after the song, Numinor and Atalanta walked with Ari and Chase up and down the rainbow. Ari greeted each of the Rainbow herd in turn; each bowed to her and to Chase, calling him "brother" and Ari "sister." Finally, with the sun at its height, Atalanta bid the Rainbow herd disperse, and the Celestial unicorns disbanded and went off to graze and play near the water.

Ari's eyes were wide with wonder, and her heart was overflowing with the beauty of it all. Atalanta regarded her quietly. Then she said, "There is one more task before us. After that, you must return to Balinor. And to battle."

Ari drew her magnificent veil around her shoulders. She knew better than to ask the Dream-speaker for a few more hours in this wonderful Valley. She was lucky, she decided, just to be here at all.

"The Watching Pool," Chase said. "Where we will learn what will come."

Atalanta nodded. "The Watching Pool is a long walk from here, Arianna. You may want to ride."

Without a word, Chase knuckled his forelegs under himself and settled onto the ground. Ari slipped onto his back. He rose, forelegs first, then his hindquarters. Then the three of them crossed the meadow to the Imperial River. Atalanta jumped gracefully into the water, and Chase followed. Ari drew her precious veil up so it wouldn't get wet, then laughed aloud as the water swirled around her legs. It tingled, like a thousand diamondlike bubbles! Atalanta swam for a few moments, then stepped onto the opposite bank. Chase swam in a large circle before he got out of the water. He was enjoying the feel of the bubbles, too. The water streamed down his sides when they climbed up the bank. By the time they reached the path that led up to the amethyst glitter Ari had seen from the arch, he was dry.

They walked up the path in the sunshine. A group of baby unicorns bounced down the side of the hill and passed them. The largest one, no bigger than Lincoln, stopped and greeted them shyly. "Hello!"

Chase stopped. Ari bent down and ran her fingers through the colt's curly mane. It felt like the softest cotton.

"Run along now, Devi," Atalanta said, and the little foal bounced away, followed by the others.

"They're all gray," Ari marveled.

"They will get their color in time," Atalanta said. "When they take their place in the rainbow."

Ari watched them happily.

"Come," Atalanta said.

The path to the Watching Pool seemed all too short. Ari didn't think she could have seen anything more marvelous than the Celestial Valley and the Rainbow herd lined up under the arch, but at the sight of the Watching Pool she almost gasped aloud. The pool was perfectly round and made of a deep violet amethyst rock. A waterfall fed the pool with a gentle rush. The waters of the pool were deep, still, and the most beautiful turquoise color Ari had ever seen.

"Dismount, and bring the Scepter forward," Atalanta said. Ari slid off Chase, and they both walked to the edge of the pool. Ari held the Scepter out.

"Dip it into the pool three times," Atalanta said. "And each time, call on the Sunchaser."

Puzzled, Ari dipped the unicorn head into the water as Atalanta had told her to do: "I call on the Sunchaser," she said each time. To her own ears, her voice sounded meek and small in the vast stillness of the pool.

At a nod from the Dreamspeaker, Chase stepped forward and his ebony horn touched the pool's surface. Three times his horn dipped down, and three times he said, "Arianna."

Ari felt a great wash of tenderness and love flow out of her and to her unicorn. It was like the course of a mighty river, enveloping them both. The Scepter glowed brightly as this feeling of the bond increased.

Then the glow from the Scepter dimmed. The flow of love and energy ebbed. "Well!" the unicorn head on the Scepter said. "It's about time!"

"Why . . . you're back!" Ari said, astonished. "I haven't heard you say a word since we visited Dr. Bohnes!"

"I never left," the unicorn head said crossly.

"But you and Sunchaser had to complete the bonding before I came into my full powers, and now you have, so let's go home."

There was a smile in Atalanta's voice. "And so you must, Scepter. But you'll allow me a word with Her Highness, won't you?"

"I suppose so," the Scepter grumbled. "But make it quick. We have a lot of work to do."

Ari bit back a giggle. The Scepter was its familiar grouchy self!

Atalanta sighed. "Yes, you do. Arianna, you now have all you need to work your own magic. It is a magic of your very own self. It is magic that rises from all that is within you."

"Within me?"

"You are the daughter of a King and Queen. A Princess in your own right. You are protected by those who live in the Celestial Valley, and bonded to one of our own." She nodded gravely at Chase. "Your magic flows from you through the Scepter and from there to the world. This magic will allow you to do what you must to lead your people well and truly. It will also allow you to make choices or do things that are wrongful, or will harm the innocent. It can be used for evil. It can be used for good. Do you understand?"

Ari was afraid to say no. But she was more afraid to tell a lie. She took a deep breath. "I don't think I do understand, Dreamspeaker."

"The power of the magic is your personal

power. You are the magic, Arianna. You are not more than the magic, you are not less. The magic is a force like that of water. You direct the water's path. You determine how the magic will be used. To use the magic, you must know yourself. You must ask questions if you are to know yourself."

Ari, bewildered and a little frightened, looked helplessly at Chase.

"She'll get it," the Scepter said impatiently. "Her mother did! We have to go, Dreamspeaker. There are terrible problems in Balinor."

Atalanta nodded. "You must listen, Ari. You must ask questions. And above all, you must learn." She raised her head so that her mane cascaded to her knees. Her tail flagged high and proud. "I can see into the future, my Princess. Not enough to forecast victory, but enough to help you a little. This I know: The Shifter will attack Balinor on the night of the Shifter's Moon. And there is worse news! He can see you now, as I see into Balinor. But his Watching Bowl will shatter, and for a time you will be safe. But each time you use your magic, he will be able to feel it. So use the Scepter only in great need, and use your own wits first." Her fine head dropped sadly. "And now, Sunchaser, I have words for you."

"I will hear them, Dreamspeaker, and will not forget." Chase dropped his muzzle on Ari's shoulder and breathed lightly into her hair while he listened.

"Rednal and Toby are losing their immortality. That is the price they pay to help you in Balinor.

But soon they *must* return to the Celestial Valley. If they do not . . ." She did not speak. But an image came to Ari's mind: the Long Green Road, the path all mortals traveled at the end of life. She shivered, wrapping the veil around her for protection.

"And do not forget your Royal brothers, Sunchaser. You must reclaim them from their sanctuary." Atalanta looked at them both. Ari bit her lip. The Royal unicorns had fled when the Shifter conquered her people. But where had they gone?

Atalanta leaned close to Ari, and her breath was sweet. "Return now, Arianna. Return to Balinor. The Shifter sulks in Castle Entia. There is half the usual number of guards at the Royal Palace. Take back your throne. And when the right time comes, call on us. We will come to help you, wherever you are. The Rainbow herd is yours to command."

Ari looked deep into Atalanta's violet eyes. The Scepter made an impatient "humph!" and said, "Mount! Mount! Time's wasting!"

Ari felt as if she were in a dream. She climbed on Chase's back, the Scepter clutched tightly in one hand.

"Into the Watching Pool!" the Scepter shouted. "Come on! We have no time to waste!"

Chase waded into the Watching Pool. Ari held her breath. They sank below the surface, the water cool and dark around them. There was a moment of confusion, of light, then dark, and then with a mighty thrust of his hindquarters, Chase swam to the surface again. Ari floated off his back and swam beside him. She came out of the water clutching Chase's mane in one hand and the Scepter in the other. She scrambled to stand up on the pebbly shore. She shook the water out of her eyes and looked up at the nighttime sky. An ordinary moon hung there, shedding almost no light. There were growls and shouts from the near shore. The lake! They were back at the lake. "Finn!" Ari shouted. "Linc!"

Her collie growled in answer. Ari pushed her hair from her eyes. Dark figures struggled back and forth on the shore. In the fitful light from the moon she saw a gleam of red hair — Finn! — and the flash of a sword. Lincoln dove and snapped at the mis-shapen creatures hitting them.

Her friends were under attack!

3

"**C**hase!" Ari cried. "We have to help them!" But the giant unicorn was already racing to the shore. Ari plunged after him, the water dragging at her boots. Chase leaped into the fray. Using his ebony horn like a sword, he charged straight at the dark thing that held Lincoln by the neck. Shrieking with fear, the attacker bolted at the sight of a huge bronze four-footed warrior.

Lori was screaming like a wild woman. One of the enemy had her by the hair, dragging her backward into the woods.

Ari's first impulse was to use the Scepter like a club. But Atalanta's words came back to her. *The power is in you! You must ask questions!*

Ari stopped. Precious seconds fled by while she watched what was happening. She fought the impulse to wade into battle. But where would her own attack be most effective? She had to see what was happening. That was it! She needed to see! She held the Scepter up and commanded, "Light!"

The Scepter responded instantly. A white flare of light spread out from the unicorn head, illuminating the scene before her. Finn struggled with a dwarfish soldier dressed in the black leather battle uniform of the Shifter's army. Lori whacked at a second soldier. Lincoln and Chase battled a Shadow unicorn with flaming eyes. Two more soldiers ripped open the saddlebags piled in a heap on the shore.

The sudden flood of bright light froze them into startled immobility. The Shifter's forces! Ari held her own fear at bay. The Shadow forces of the Shifter feared bright light. *If it were bright enough,* Ari thought, *I could scare them away!*

And the Scepter responded to her thought! In no more than an instant, the white light became so intense that Ari had to squeeze her eyes shut. The light was blinding, painful, and a hundred times brighter than the sun at noon. The soldiers screamed; the Shadow unicorns roared with rage. Ari heard the thud of running feet, and then Lori's angry shout, "Turn that light off!"

"Ari, is that you?" Finn called.

Lincoln whined. A dog's eyes were very sensitive, Ari knew, and she said urgently, "Turn off, Scepter!" But the light continued to throb brightly, the Scepter heedless of Ari's command. Desperate, Ari plunged the Scepter headfirst into the water. The

29

Scepter yelped, and the light went out abruptly. Ari opened her eyes cautiously. Now everything was too dark! She couldn't see a thing! She stumbled forward and found Chase standing at the shoreline. He nudged her shoulder with his muzzle. *Good try, milady!* he thought at her.

It worked, Chase. But I'm not sure how! And I have no idea how to do it again! She blinked a few times, and her sight returned to normal. She pulled the Scepter out of the water and waded toward shore.

"Don't ever do that again!" the Scepter scolded. "You could have drowned me!"

"*Now* you turn up," Lori said crossly. "It's just like you to go waltzing off when you're needed! Some Princess you are!"

"Lori!" Finn said in an urgent undertone. "You can't talk to Her Royal — I mean Ari that way."

"I can talk to her any way I please," Lori said, tossing her blond head.

"You might try thanking Ari for saving our skins," Lincoln said. He sat down with a thump and began to lick his white forepaws clean. "We weren't doing too well holding them off until she showed up with the magic."

"Humph!" Lori muttered under her breath. She flounced over to the saddlebags and began to sort through the mess the soldiers had made of their contents.

"Are you all okay?" Ari asked Finn. She held

30

him by the shoulders and looked keenly into his face. He'd obviously been in a fight; there was a huge bruise on his right cheek and a scratch on his forehead. "What happened?"

"Well, after you and Chase disappeared into the sky, there was nothing to do but wait. We were pretty sure you were coming back — at least Lincoln and I were — but you were gone a long time. We made that fire and settled in to spend the night. I must have fallen asleep, because the next thing I knew, some thug was slapping me around, telling me to give it to him, give it to him, and Lincoln was barking up a storm, and then all of a sudden you came out of the lake with this great blazing light in one hand . . . and you know the rest. I think they were after the Royal Scepter." He stopped a moment, then said shyly, "You looked beautiful, with that red veil and the light spilling all over you from the Scepter."

"Well! They didn't take anything, but they sure made a mess of my clothes," Lori snarled. She sat down next to Ari and Finn with a thud. "So, where were you when we needed you?"

Ari hesitated, mindful of Atalanta's warning not to tell anyone of her visit to the Celestial Valley. "It doesn't matter where Chase and I were," she said. "Just that we got back in time to give you a little help."

"I see you finally decided to stop being stuck up about it and use the magic," Lori said. "Although you weren't especially good at it. You could have blinded us with that light! What's the matter with you, anyway? Who's in charge, anyhow? You or the magic?"

It almost killed Ari to apologize, but Lori was right. She hadn't controlled the magic very well. "I've got a lot to learn, I think," she said. "I'm sorry. As a matter of fact . . ." She broke off what she was saying and gazed at the Scepter. She would not use it again. Not unless the need was overwhelming. It was too risky — and besides, the Shifter could feel the magic. And if he could feel it, he could find her. And until she and the rest of Balinor were ready to fight, she didn't want to meet up with him and his grisly Shadow unicorns unprepared! "As a matter of fact, I won't use it the rest of this trip."

"Fine by me," Lori grumbled. "Fine thing if you get us all killed!"

"Let's leave it at that," Ari said firmly. "And from the look of the eastern horizon, the sun will soon be up, and we've got to get back to Balinor. Let's get some breakfast and be on our way."

Grumbling, Lori took herself off and began to sort through the overturned saddlebags for the container of oatmeal and berry syrup they carried with them. Finn went to tend the fire. Ari stood up, took the gorgeous red velvet veil from around her shoulders, and folded it carefully. She was glad that Atalanta had allowed her to keep it. It might even have many small bits of magic worked into the elegant fabric. It was neither wet nor torn after her

32

swim in the lake and her battle with the Shifter's soldiers.

"Ari? The others couldn't see, but I did," Lincoln said in a wistful way. He gazed up at her, his
deep brown eyes sorrowful. "You saw her, didn't
you? Atalanta. The Twilight Mare. The Lady of the
Moon."

Ari nodded silently.

"They held the Celestial Ceremony of Bonding. And you were there, in the valley!"

The longing in his voice touched Ari's heart.
She knelt beside him and ran her hands affectionately through his thick white ruff. "You aren't supposed to know these things, Linc. How do you know
these things?" She held his face between her hands.
She loved her collie, with his thick mahogany-and-
cream coat and beautiful triangular face. But she remembered something she had known long ago —
when she was in hiding, just Ari the stable girl at
Glacier River Farm on the other side of the Gap,
and Linc was the farm dog in charge of herding
the horses there. No one — not her foster parents,
or her guardian-nurse, Dr. Bohnes, or Atalanta
herself — had known where Lincoln came from. He
had appeared one day, and that was that. All his
love, all his loyalty was for Ari — but where he was
from, or what he had been before, was unknown.

"Linc," Ari said to him, "now that I have all I
need to use the Royal magic . . ." But Ari never finished what she was about to say. Lori stamped over

33

and informed her curtly that the breakfast oatmeal was ready. Finn was right behind her, anxious to get started on the way home to Balinor.

They ate a hasty breakfast — Lori had reserved uncooked oatmeal for the unicorns, who preferred it that way — then repacked the saddlebags. In less than an hour they were back on the path to Balinor.

Ari and Finn jogged silently side by side. Rednal and Chase spoke little to each other, only to remark on the ruts in the road, or the morning heat. Lori brought up the rear, squabbling with Toby about his stiff-legged trot.

The thick trees of Ardit soon gave way to farmland, and farmland to an occasional thatched cottage where the workers lived. They had seen no more of the Shifter's forces since the brief attack by the shore of the lake, but Ari knew their good luck wouldn't last. On the top of a small rise that led down to a well-used road, Ari drew rein and said, "We need to talk about what we're going to do."

The others gathered around in a circle. Ari looked at them. They were such good friends! They had been through so much together in Ari's quest to regain the throne of Balinor and free her people from the evil Shifter. And now she had to ask for their help again! "Good people," Ari began.

"Stop that," Lori said crossly. "Don't call us your 'good people.' We decided that we were all in this together, and we're stuck with it, I guess. And I know what you're going to say. We've got to charge the palace and try to throw the Shifter's guards out of it. Right?"

"Right," Ari said.

"So what's the plan? Do we go back to the Unicorn Inn and get Samlett and the Lords of Balinor to raise an army?" Lori asked impatiently.

"There's no time for that," Ari said. "Any time we take to gather our forces, the Shifter has to gather his forces. We know that he's at Castle Entia in the Valley of Fear, because that's where we left him. I found out last night. . . ." She hesitated, afraid to say too much. "Anyway, I know that there are only a few guards at the palace now. About half a platoon or so. We need to charge the palace — now."

Lori gulped. "Now? Without a whole army behind us?"

"If we take time to gather an army, so will the Shifter. The more people involved in this, the more chance there is of . . ."

Nobody wanted her to say it, so she didn't. But they all knew what she meant. The greater the numbers, the greater the injuries and wounds.

"What should we do, Ari?" Finn asked. His hand went to his sword. "I'll defend you to the death!"

"And I!" Rednal said, and Toby grunted his agreement.

Trust in yourself, Chase reminded her through his thoughts. *Trust in me!*

"We're going to ride through the village and up to the palace itself," Ari said steadily. "I will wear the veil given to me by the Dreamspeaker. And I will carry THIS!" She took the Scepter from her belt and held it high. "We will call the people to our cause. We will ride — with those who volunteer with us — to the gates of the palace and reclaim it for our own!"

4

❦

Red fires burned low in the pits and hollows of the Valley of Fear. The desert sand was harsh and hot under a gloomy sun. Soaring over it all were the cold stone walls and cruel towers of Castle Entia, home of the evil Shifter. In the black granite court-yard, an army of leather-clad soldiers and Shadow unicorns shuffled torpidly in the heat. They had re-turned in force to the Valley of Fear at their master's call — and the rumors about why they were assem-bled flew among the troops like so many carrion birds. All knew part of the truth — that Princess Ari-anna and her great bronze unicorn, the Sunchaser, had returned to Balinor. And with their return, there would be war.

From his corner tower, the Shifter gazed down at his troops. Today he was a giant black bat. Wings folded closely to his sides, he hung upside down at his window. The only things visible in his shadowy form were his burning eyes.

"The Princessss approachessss the palace," a voice hissed behind him.

The Shifter's eyes narrowed to flaming slits. The voice belonged to his chief advisor, Lady Kylie. She had been useful once, in those long-ago days when the rightful King and Queen ruled Balinor and the Princess Arianna had been a sapphire-eyed toddler. Kylie had been the Queen of Balinor's best friend — and secretly, her greatest enemy. On the day of the Great Betrayal, it was Kylie who had told Entia — the Shifter — the secrets of the palace. Armed with this knowledge, the Shifter had kidnapped the King and Queen and their sons, the Princes, and taken control of Balinor. The cursed Dreamspeaker had helped send Arianna and the Sunchaser to safety on the other side of the Gap; until Arianna and her unicorn had returned, the Shifter had ruled without question.

But all was different now. The Princess was back and in full control of her personal magic. The Royal magic! And the Shifter's reign of terror was in jeopardy.

"Come look!" Kylie insisted behind him.

With a hiss of anger, Entia shifted from his bat form into the guise of a huge, black-bearded man. His wings flowed into arms. His hind claws transformed into booted feet. He landed on the stone floor of the tower with an angry thud, then turned and walked into the center of the chamber.

Kylie stood before a tall pedestal that held a large bowl. She was half-woman, half-snake, and she swayed back and forth on her scaly tail, looking into the bowl. Entia shoved her aside and looked into the bowl himself.

Like the magic waters of the Watching Pool in the Celestial Valley, the water in this bowl also held images of faraway places. But these waters were muddy, bloodred, and stagnant.

"Curse her!" Entia muttered as he stared into the bowl. The image of the Princess and her friends was clear enough. Arianna and the Sunchaser rode rapidly through the streets of Balinor. A long red veil flowed from her shoulders and swept over the thickly muscled hindquarters of her Bonded partner. Arianna's bronze hair mingled with the silver embroidery on the cloak. Her brilliant blue eyes were steely with determination. She held the Royal Scepter high. Behind her were Finn and Rednal, Lori and Toby, and the magnificent collie, Lincoln. And behind them . . .

The people of Balinor! As the Princess and her friends continued on, the villagers came out and followed. They opened the doors of their houses and shops and joined the procession. Some carried clubs, others long staves, rakes, or hoes — or anything that could serve as a weapon.

Arianna reached the bend in the road that led to the palace. She turned in the saddle and raised the Scepter above her head so that all could see. A great sweep of light came from the unicorn head atop the Scepter, illuminating unicorn and rider. "Good people!" Her voice was clear and strong. "For my mother! For my father! For my brothers! For Balinor!" Sunchaser whinnied a war cry. And the crowd cheered, a mighty cheer that seemed to shake the very foundations of Entia's castle, although the Shifter knew it could not be so.

The taking of the palace was quick. The small company of guards the Shifter had left in charge ran away even before Arianna reached the broad palace steps. Ari and Chase crossed the footbridge over the moat, went through the vast wooden doors, and up the sweeping white stairway.

The Royal Palace was theirs!

With a curse, the Shifter swept the bowl to the tower floor. It shattered into a thousand pieces. Muddy water sprayed everywhere. Kylie squirmed away with a whining hiss. The Shifter paced back and forth, his hobnailed boots clicking ominously.

"It issss not sssso much of a victory," Kylie ventured after a moment. "They cannot sssstand against our army. We should gather our forcessss and attack! The brat got lucky!"

The Shifter frowned uncertainly.

"Yessss! Yesssss! You sssshall ride Moloch at the head of our faithful sssssoldiers! He is a unicorn

40

to sssstrike terror into the heartssss of all those brave citizenssss!" Her voice dripped with scorn. "They will not be so anxioussss to rally around that girl and her pitiful group of friends when they ssssee you and Moloch leading the Shadow warriors into the fight."

The Shifter thought of the huge Shadow unicorn with grim satisfaction. Kylie was right, for once. It had been a long time since she had been right — hadn't he lost the Indigo Star after listening to her? And that Royal brat and her unicorn had snatched the Royal Scepter from Kylie without so much as a blow being exchanged!

But war, with Moloch and himself at the head of the army?

Perhaps Kylie was right. He stood a moment, deep in thought. No, he was ready to dispense with the snakewoman. She was no longer of use to him. He could ride — would ride — without her. Even now, the guards should be mounting the stairs outside the tower. As soon as he had discovered she'd failed to retrieve the Royal Scepter, he had ordered them to take her and fling her into prison. He cocked his head. Yes! There was the sound of someone coming up the stairs!

ONE! The iron stairs clanged with a heavy tread.

Kylie hissed nervously and twisted her fingers in her snaky black hair.

TWO! The guard had mounted a second step.

41

"I know what you're trying to do," Kylie said. Her forked red tongue flickered in and out of her scarlet mouth. "You think you're so ssssmart, Sssshifter. But you aren't, you know . . ."

THREE! The iron door burst open. The expectant grin died on the Shifter's lips. For no stunted, misshapen guard stumbled into the room. Instead, a tall, cowled figure stood before him. The hood covering his face was deep, but the Shifter knew what terrible thing lay inside:

The Shadow Rider!

"Begone!" Entia growled softly. "You have no business here!"

A cold breeze stirred the Rider's cloak, but there was no answer.

"Ssssend him away!" Kylie whispered urgently. "He is a sssspy!"

"A spy for whom?" Entia demanded. "You fool! This one rides for evil, not for good! I have summoned him to help us before!" Entia's eyes narrowed slyly. "Although he wasn't much use, I'll give you that."

Kylie's forked tongue darted in and out of her mouth. She swayed on her thick, snaky tail. "He issss dangeroussss, I tell you!"

Instantly, Entia shifted into a huge, winged unicorn. His horn was a deadly spear of iron, his hooves sharp and dangerous. And his teeth were fanged, the better to rend and tear at an enemy. He reared up and his forelegs pawed the air in challenge. He landed on all four hooves with a bellow of rage. "Now who's dangerous?" he asked mockingly. "Begone, Rider! I will summon you — if and when I need you!"

For a second, the Rider seemed to shrink in size. His hood merged into his shoulders. Slowly, under the muffling folds of his cloak, he raised both arms to shoulder height. He shrank farther and farther down. The cloak spread wider.

The Shifter stamped his hooves uneasily.

"So you think that shifting will save you?" the Rider asked. "But *I* can do that, too!" The hooded figure shook with laughter. The Rider looked like a giant toadstool, covered with that spreading black cloak. The horrible shape advanced jerkily. His arms had become legs! Many legs! Under the cover of the cloak, the Rider had shifted his shape!

Entia stared at it, his eyes narrowed. "How is it," he asked coldly, "how *is* it, Kylie, that this creature can use the shifting magic?" He whirled and glared at her. "What have you done? If you have betrayed me or my magic, you will regret it for the rest of your miserable days!"

Kylie backed away. She raised her arm and pointed shakily at the wall. Entia turned back to the spot where the Rider had been squatting not seconds before.

The cloak was a puddle of cloth on the stones. The Rider was gone!

"Up!" Kylie screamed. "Look up!"

The Shifter raised his head. His heart jumped in his chest. A giant spider inched its way across the ceiling. It had eight hairy legs, each ending in a terrible spike. A horrible green slime oozed from its beak. It chittered; the upper and lower half of its beak sliced open and shut with the "snick" of two knife blades clashing together.

"You!" the Shifter said. He scowled. "My liege, Kraken!"

"Kraken!" Kylie wriggled on the floor in abject fear. She had heard tales of this evil being from the Deep Magic. But Kraken was as seldom seen as his own sworn enemy, the Old Mare of the Mountain.

The Shifter ground his teeth in rage. He had been tricked! All this time he had believed that the Shadow Rider was under his control! And all this time the Rider had been Kraken!

Swiftly, Entia shifted from his unicorn shape to that of a man again. He dropped to one knee and bent his head. Whatever tricky game Kraken was up to, the Shifter knew he was no match for the evil from the Deep Magic. The only consolation the Shifter could find was that that cursed Princess and her Dreamspeaker couldn't control the Old Mare of the Mountain, either. Beings from the Deep Magic explained themselves to no one. Entia bowed lower than before and tried to control the fear in his voice. "My liege," he said again, "I had no idea that you had graced us with your presence this far! If I had known . . ."

"If you had known, would you have kept the Indigo Star? Not lost the Royal Scepter?" The spider paused and looked down at the Shifter with its single yellow-green eye. "Oh, Entia!" Kraken's voice was horrible, thin and rank. "You have one more chance, Entia!" Kraken's yellow-green eye winked at him in a hideous parody of friendship. "One more chance to defeat the Princess and her unicorn in battle! If you lose . . ." The spider crawled on, giggling. The giggle was like the hiss of air escaping from a balloon. "If you lose . . ."

The hideous spider crawled out the window and disappeared. The cloak on the stone floor disintegrated in a stinking puff of smoke.

"Issss he gone?" Kylie quavered from the floor.

"Get up!" he snarled. "And shed that snakeskin, Kylie! There is work for you to do!" He took three strides across the room and flung the iron door wide. He screamed with fury.

In the courtyard below, his soldiers heard his shriek of rage and shivered in their leather jerkins. A coal-black unicorn with fiery eyes bared his teeth in a fierce grin and nodded to his herdmates. The Shadow unicorns jostled one another expectantly.

"Arianna!" the Shifter shouted. His huge voice echoed hollowly against the cold stone walls of Castle Entia. "Arianna! It is war!"

5

"Ari! This was your room when you were a kid?" Lori said. She stared openmouthed at the rose-pink marble floor. Ari's old room was on the third level of the palace, facing the flower gardens. Glass doors led to a huge wraparound balcony. Lori could see fountains, paths of crushed stone winding between glorious shrubbery, and a huge bathing pool in the gardens below the balcony.

Inside, one whole wall was a fireplace of the same pink marble that covered the floor. Beautiful carvings of vines and fruits covered the mantel. A low fire burned in the grate, sending the sweet scent of applewood into the air. A four-poster bed stood in one corner, draped with curtains of deep pink silk. In the opposite corner was a carved screen that hid a gold bathtub and a gold mirror. Gorgeously carved wooden chests were scattered throughout the room.

Huge cushiony pillows lay heaped on the bed and on the floor.

Ari sat cross-legged on a damask cushion in front of the fireplace. Lincoln was curled next to her, and she absentmindedly combed his white ruff. She didn't answer Lori's incredulous question.

Lori glared at her, then lifted the lid to one of the chests. It was filled with beautiful clothes: a sky-blue underskirt with a silver brocade tunic; a deep amber cloak with heavy gold embroidery; a velvet riding habit trimmed with white swan feathers. Ari had carefully folded the red velvet veil Atalanta had given her and put it in the trunk. Lori let the lid drop with a slam. "Well!" she said sarcastically. "It must be nice to be home!"

Lori heard a timid knock on the huge logan-wood door that led from Ari's bedroom to the hall outside. The sound didn't break Ari's concentration. The knock sounded again, more urgently. Lori heaved a huge theatrical sigh, then flounced to the door and opened it. Runetta, the Innkeeper's wife, stood there, as round and rosy as ever. "What do you want?" Lori demanded.

Runetta peered past Lori's shoulder. "Is Her Royal Highness in?"

"See for yourself!" Lori stepped back. Runetta bustled forward and sank to her knees with a glad cry. "Princess! You have returned! The entire village is rejoicing!"

Ari turned around with a jerk and leaped to her feet. "Runetta!" she cried. She grasped the good woman by both hands and pulled her to her feet. "I'm so glad to see you! And how is your good husband, Samlett?"

"Samlett is fine! And I have missed *you*, milady!" She gave Ari a tremendous hug, then held her at arm's length. "Now, just look at you!" she scolded fondly. "You look like something the cat dragged in!"

Lincoln growled.

"Now, Lincoln, you know what I mean. Princess, Princess!" She shook her head. "Your hair is filled with twigs and your face is dirty, and your *clothes*!" She shook her head harder at the sight of Ari's tattered skirt and worn-out boots. "We'll have to get you into a bath and some fresh clothes!"

"Hello!" Lori said. "I'm not exactly squeaky clean myself here! What about me?"

Runetta spared a brief glance for Lori, then clucked her tongue. "Well, you can't meet the Lords of Balinor in such a state, milady. I'll call the servants to draw a bath for you, and we'll get you some food."

"Please find something for Lincoln to eat," Ari said. Her voice was tired. "And I'll need a brush and a comb, Runetta, if you could be so good. His fur is a mess."

"Your Royal Highness is NOT going to waste time on the dog. I'll find someone to do it for you."

She looked around the chamber and finally seemed to see Lori. "Here, my girl, you take care of the dog, while I attend to Her Royal Highness."

"I am *not* giving that dog a bath!" Lori shouted. "Do I look like a dog-washer?"

"Hey!" Lincoln said uneasily. He didn't approve of baths for dogs. "What's this bath stuff, anyway? I don't need a bath! As a matter of fact, I was just about to go down to the stables and have a little chat with Chase!" He trotted hopefully to the door. Ari grabbed his ruff just in time.

"And I would just like to know," Lori interrupted them all, "why no one is paying attention to me! *I'm* just as grubby and hungry as Her Royal High and Mightiness!"

"No one's paying attention to you because you aren't important," Lincoln said rudely.

"Oh, yeah?" Lori put her hands on her hips and stuck out her lower lip.

Lincoln lowered his head and growled, "Yeah!"

"Stop it, please," Ari said in a soft voice. "Runetta! I'm so glad you are here! But I don't need your help to get bathed and changed."

"Your Royal Highness!" Runetta gasped, scandalized. "Of course you do! You haven't any of your ladies-in-waiting to attend to you. And you certainly can't do it yourself!"

"I most certainly can." Ari's voice was kind,

but firm. "I have to meet with the Lords Puckenstew, Artos, and Rexel, don't I?"

"They are waiting for you in the Grand Hall."

"I don't want to keep them waiting much longer. If you could prepare us all some food, it would speed things up. It would just waste time if you waited on me. We're all so hungry, Runetta! I hate to ask you, but I'm afraid the kitchens aren't open yet. And, of course, all the cooks ran away when the Shifter took over the palace."

"You should see those kitchens! Those guards of the Shifter left a mess and a half, I can tell you! That stove!" Runetta rolled her eyes. "That stove hasn't been cleaned since . . ." She stopped, then faltered on. "I mean, your Royal mother would just die. . . ." Runetta burst into tears. "I'm sorry, Princess! I didn't mean to remind you!"

"Of the day of the Great Betrayal? Of the fact that my mother and father and brothers are still missing? I didn't need reminding, Runetta. All this . . ." She waved her hand to indicate the beautiful room and the gardens beyond. "All this brings back the most painful memories! I miss them so much, Runetta."

The kindly woman enveloped Ari in a gentle hug. Even Lori felt Ari's grief. She walked over and patted Ari awkwardly on the back.

Ari wiped her eyes with the back of her sleeve. "It'll get a lot tougher if we don't plan to get my parents back," she said in a practical way. "Now,

Runetta, please see if you can put together a nice meal for the lords and for Lori, Finn, and Linc. The three of us here will meet you in the Great Hall in about thirty minutes."

Happy with something comforting to do, Runetta bustled off, but not before she unearthed a wooden comb and brush for Lincoln from one of the chests.

Ari went to the gold bathtub and turned the tap on. Water flowed out, and Lori came to look. "You've got plumbing here?"

Ari smiled a little. She frequently forgot that Lori was from the other side of the Gap. "Our land must seem very different to you from Glacier River Farm," she said. "But of course we have plumbing here! There is a system of wooden pipes that runs through the palace. The water comes in from the river."

Lori swished her hands in the rapidly filling tub. "Yikes! It's *cold!*"

"There's a whole group of people who bring hot water from the kitchens below," Ari said with a smile. "When the palace is up and running, we'll be able to fill those jobs again. But for right now . . ." She laughed. "Sorry. But it's better to be cold and clean than warm and dirty!"

Lori wasn't sure she agreed. Ari brushed and combed Lincoln while Lori bathed, then draped a lovely pale green dress and tunic over the wooden screen for her to wear. Then Ari cleaned herself up and dressed in a modest brown velvet skirt with a cream linen blouse and a leather vest. Her one extravagance was a pair of soft leather boots. The leather was so fine and supple that Lori gasped.

"I'm afraid that my boots won't fit you," Ari said. "But you can wear these sandals." She held up a pair of pretty rope sandals that tied with silk ribbons. This made them easy to fit Lori's feet, which were wider than Ari's. "There's a Royal bootmaker, or there used to be. We'll have to ask him to make you a pair of shoes."

Finally, Ari took the Royal Scepter in hand. They were ready. Ari led the way down the huge sweeping staircase to the second floor, where the Royal apartments were, and then to the first floor, where the Royal family received guests.

Ari was dismayed. Everything was a mess. Mud and trash were everywhere. But Runetta had already recruited villagers to help clean up. Ari held back her anger at the damage done by the Shifter's evil army, greeting those who were sweeping and washing with a smile and a kind word. Every time a villager curtsied to Ari, or called, "Bless you, milady!" Lori grumbled under her breath.

But Ari pushed aside any thoughts about Lori. She had an important job ahead: She had to convince those Lords of Balinor still loyal to the King and Queen that she was in fact the Princess Arianna. She had the certificate from her dear Dr. Bohnes. It didn't really help to have the Royal

Scepter — the Shifter himself had stolen it once. The Scepter was part of the Deep Magic; the one who wielded it could channel its energy. She hoped that the certificate from her old nurse would be enough.

The towering wooden doors to the Great Hall were closed. Finn waited there for her. He was wearing a fresh white shirt and had made an attempt to clean his leather breeches and boots. His red hair was damp and stuck out around his ears. Ari was very glad to see him. She was a bit nervous about facing the Lords of Balinor again, and the more friends she had around her, the better.

"Chase took Rednal and Toby out to the Royal mews to find out what happened to the Royal unicorns," Finn greeted her. "He should be here pretty soon."

Ari nodded. "He's on his way."

Finn looked a little sheepish. Ari and Chase were a Bonded Pair; of course she would always know where her unicorn was! Sure enough, they heard the clatter of hooves on marble, and Chase led the other two unicorns up the broad front steps and into the palace.

Before she had gone up to her room with Lori, Ari had washed and brushed Chase to gleaming perfection. She had never seen him look so royal. His bronze mane flowed almost to his knees, and he flagged his tail so that it swept behind him like a silky waterfall. His ebony horn glowed a deep burnished black. On impulse, she swept him a curtsy. "Your Majesty!" she said, smiling. "You look every inch the Lord of the Animals!"

His dark brown eyes wrinkled in amusement. He looked even more royal when flanked by the two other Celestial unicorns. Rednal stood at his right. Finn had brushed his chestnut coat until it shone as red as fire. The Celestial unicorn stood at attention, his head tucked, neck arched. Toby stood at Chase's left. The stout little unicorn stood as proudly as his fellows, his black-and-white coat in sharp contrast to the magnificence of Chase's bronze glory. But he, too, was brushed and combed, and he had a stout dignity that became him well.

"We stand ready to serve you, milady!" Rednal said.

Chase stepped to Ari's side. She laid a hand on his mane and nodded to Finn. Finn thrust open the huge doors and announced:

"Her Royal Highness, the Princess Arianna! Defender of the Unicorns, and Bonded Partner to the Sunchaser!"

Ari and Chase walked into the Great Hall to meet the Lords of Balinor.

6

The Great Hall was long and narrow. The ceilings soared up and met in a peak. Large windows lined the sides, flooding the room with sunlight. The thrones were at the very end, arranged on a tallish, two-tiered pyramid made of gilded wood. The King's and Queen's thrones sat on the top platform, glittering with gold and red, the Royal colors of Balinor. One step down were the red velvet chairs for the Royal Princes and Princesses.

A long table was set in front of the thrones. Three men there sat facing Ari and her friends.

You remember them, milady? Chase sent his message to her mind.

How could I forget? she responded. As far back in Balinor history as Ari could remember, there had been Seven Great Houses. Each House was commanded by one of the Seven Lords; each maintained an army of knights ready to be called in service to the King and Queen. The Shifter had won over four of the Great Houses. Only three remained loyal to Ari and her family. But she wasn't all that sure of their loyalty!

"Maybe we should wait here for you," Lori whispered nervously. "Those guys look tough!"

"We go wherever the Princess goes," Finn said stoutly. Lincoln growled his agreement.

Ari kept her eyes on the lords at the table as she and Chase walked proudly down the hall. The big, muscular man in the middle was Puckenstew. Strong as an ox, Lord Puckenstew had never been defeated in a joust or tournament. His nickname was Lord Bear, because he had hair all over his arms, legs, and face. The round, cheery-faced man next to him was Artos; he was so short, he stood on his chair. Even then, his head barely came to the ears of the third lord.

The third lord was Rexel. Tall, gaunt, suspicious, Rexel had a mean mouth and unkind eyes. He had a reputation for driving his servants and his unicorns hard. But unlike the four lords who had defected, Rexel had remained loyal. Ari thought briefly of Lord Lexan, brother of the horrible Lady Kylie. Lexan had at last declared allegiance to the Shifter. He had seemed so kind! And he had turned into such a traitor!

Ari and Chase came to a halt in front of the table. For a moment, no one said anything. Ari noticed that Artos and Puckenstew both wore ceremonial court dress, long wool gowns with ankle-length vests of leather worked in gold and silver. But Rexel wore battle garb. Ari found this ominous, but she kept her face carefully neutral. Court protocol demanded that her subjects greet her first. She resolved not to break the silence. "Rise, milords!" Finn said boldly. "And greet Her Royal Highness with the courtesy due to her rank!"

Artos (who was standing already, so Ari wasn't sure if this counted or not) bounced on his heels and said in his high, chirpy voice: "Your Highness! It is good to see you safe at home again!"

Beside him, Puckenstew rose to his full height. He bowed from the waist. "Your journey to seek Dr. Bohnes was successful, Your Royal Highness! We are glad to see you safe at home again. And gladder still that you and your mighty unicorns have cleared the palace of the enemy! That was a good day's work!"

Rexel said, "Hmm," and didn't move at all.

Chase had been standing quietly, remote and magnificent. He bent his head. His ebony horn pointed directly at Lord Rexel. "Sir," he said in deep courteous tones, "you have not risen to greet the Princess."

"I'd like to see proof that she is the Princess!" Rexel said querulously. "We sent her off to find the old nurse and have her certified. Do you carry this missive, um . . ."

"You will address the Princess properly!" Chase thundered.

The room went quiet for a moment. Finally, Rexel muttered, "YourRoyalHighness" so quickly that it was hard to hear.

"I have the paper here." Ari drew the rolled parchment from her leather vest and laid it on the table.

"Of course, of course she's the Princess!" Artos said in his squeaky voice. "What is the matter with you, Rexel? Didn't you hear about how she swept through the palace? How the enemy ran before her and the Royal Scepter?"

Ari lifted the Scepter. Rexel got to his feet and bowed ceremoniously. "Your Royal Highness," he said in his raspy way. But Ari noticed he unrolled the parchment and read it carefully before bowing again. "It is indeed you, my Princess," he said smoothly. "We await your ascent to the throne!" He indicated the empty King's and Queen's thrones towering above him.

"I will not sit on any throne until my family has been restored to me," Ari said firmly. "That's that, gentlemen. I suggest we sit down and begin to plan immediately. We have very little time before the Shifter attacks. And we must be ready!"

Rexel, Artos, and Puckenstew bowed to her again. Ari pulled out a chair and sat down. Chase stood quietly behind her. Lincoln nudged close to her chair and settled his nose in her lap. There was a brief, uncomfortable pause, and then the lords sat down, too. Finn and Lori took chairs on either side of Ari.

Before Ari could begin, Runetta appeared at the door at the back of the thrones, carrying a large tray of food. A whole parade of helpers followed her, each carrying food or drink. "Bless my soul, bless my soul," Runetta muttered. She set the dishes down, curtsying each time she did so. Ari watched her for a minute and got dizzy. She held up her hands, laughing. "Runetta! *Please* stop curtsying!"

The kindly woman placed a platter of delicately fried, sugared dough balls in front of Ari, and then a bowl of fresh greens sprinkled with herbs and lemon. "*Not* curtsy to Your Royal Highness?" (She curtsied.) "I've never heard of such a thing!" (She curtsied again.) "After all this time, waiting for you to return to us, not to give you the respect you deserve? I've never heard of such a thing!"

Ari grabbed her elbow just as she was about to duck down for the final time. "Enough!" she commanded. "We are all in this fight against the Shifter together, Runetta! There's no time for this . . . this . . . ceremonial stuff!"

Rexel shook his head. "That is a bad mistake, Your Royal Highness."

"No official Royal balls?" Artos squeaked. "No Royal ladies-in-waiting? My wife will be so disappointed! She has a new velvet gown ordered already! She expects to resume her Royal duties as soon as possible!"

Ari shook her head.

"Wait-wait-wait-wait," Lori said. She curled a strand of blond hair around her finger in a studiously indifferent way. "A velvet gown? Ladies-in-waiting? Royal duties?"

"Her Royal Highness has several ladies-in-waiting in attendance at all times!" Runetta scolded affectionately. "Or she should, at any rate. Who ever heard of a Princess without Royal attendants!"

"These ladies-in-waiting," Lori said, "are they Royal, too?"

"Oh, yes, miss!"

"And you don't call them 'miss' or anything? They're just as good as a Princess. Maybe even better?"

Runetta took a deep breath.

Ari leaned back and eyed her friend. Poor Lori was certainly suffering from lack of things to do! She was scared to fight, afraid of the dark, squeamish about roughing it when they went on long journeys, and far too jealous of Ari's role. Ari had told Lori often enough that being the Princess was hard and lonesome — but Lori never saw past the glitter and glamour on the outside to the terrifying responsibilities inside. "Very well," Ari said. Everyone instantly became quiet. "I shall appoint two ladies-in-waiting. I don't need any more than that." She wanted none at all, but she didn't say that aloud. "Each shall have a clothes allowance and a title. Let's say, that would be . . . um . . . Lady Lori of Balinor — that's you, Lori."

Lori clapped her hands in excitement. "And who is the other one?"

"We can decide that later, Lori."

"How *much* of a clothes allowance do I get?" Lori asked. "Is it a lot?"

"It'll be enough," Ari said firmly. "I just haven't decided yet."

"Thank you, milady, for settling that very important point!" Lord Rexel rose to his feet and bowed, a little sarcastically, Ari thought. "Now, perhaps, we can plan what we are going to do about the Shifter!"

Ari bowed back. "Now," she agreed, "we must plan." She set the platters of food aside and folded her hands on the table. "The Shifter will attack us on the first night of the Shifter's Moon. And we must be ready."

She waited patiently for the furor her words caused to die down. When all was again quiet, she looked up at Chase. He sent her a warm, loving thought, then she said to the others, "We have very little time. Two weeks at most. The Silver Traveler, as all animals in Balinor call the moon, is full tonight. In fourteen days, she will go dark. And the first of three nights of the Shifter's Moon will begin. Those are the nights when there is no moon and the sky is dark and lonely, when the Shifter's power is at its height!"

"I will have all my knights at your disposal, milady!" Puckenstew shouted. He was so excited, a bit of soup ran into his beard. He dabbed at it with his napkin. "I have forty men-at-arms! All armed and ready to fight!"

"And their unicorns?" Chase asked gravely. "Are they ready to fight as well? They are not. They have fled. And you have made no push to find them, Lord Puckenstew!"

This time the silence around the table was stricken and grave. When the Shifter had first attacked Balinor and kidnapped the Royal family, all the Royal unicorns had fled, rather than be captured and forced into slavery in the Shifter's army. A very few remained — some had hidden from the Shifter's army successfully for a long time — but they were scattered all over the place.

"I had forgotten about the unicorns," Lord Puckenstew said sadly.

"I see unicorns all over Balinor," Lori said. "Why don't you just ask them to help?"

"You don't understand, Lori," Finn began.

"Lady Lori," Lori said. "You can't just call me Lori anymore. I'm a lady-in-waiting."

"Sorry," Finn said. He grinned. "Okay, *Lady* Lori. There are four kinds of unicorns. You see the Balinor Worker unicorns every day. They are friends to humans, and they help us work. We ride them to

62

town, they volunteer to pull carriages, and they help us transport food and other things from place to place. Then there are the Royals. You've seen only a few of them, perhaps. The jewel at the base of their horns is a precious stone. All unicorns carry their personal magic in the jewels at the base of their horns — but the Royal unicorn's magic is powerful. They are warriors and they serve the Royal family directly, as do Lord Puckenstew and Lord Artos. And Lord Rexel, of course. These are the unicorns who have been scattered because of the Shifter's evil."

"Oh." Lori nibbled at a grain muffin. "You said there are more kinds of unicorns."

"Why, the Celestial unicorns, of course!" Runetta broke in. "Even you should know that, my child, although you are a foreigner."

Lori scowled. "I'm not a foreigner, I'm a lady-in-waiting. And you forgot to call me —"

"Lady Lori," Chase interrupted firmly. "The Celestial unicorns are herdmates of the Dream-speaker."

"Well, I've never seen any!" Lori said.

Ari opened her mouth, astonished at her friend's ignorance. Why, Lori had ridden Toby all over Balinor during their adventures!

NO! Chase's thought was so intense, Ari nearly fell over. *I'm sorry, milady. But do not reveal Rednal and Toby to this company!*

Ari, bewildered, thought back, *Why? These are our allies!*

They are. But we must be careful. The fewer who know that Rednal and Toby are Celestials, the safer they will be. What if, somehow, the Shifter were to capture them?

You're right. We must be both careful and watchful, Chase!

"Ari!" Lori demanded.

Ari came to herself with a start.

"What's Chase?"

"Chase?" Ari reached up and stroked his mane. "Chase is Lord of the Animals in Balinor, Lori. While he is here among us, he is Royal. But he is kin to the Dreamspeaker and her kind. Celestial unicorns are immortal, you know. When they descend the Crystal Arch —"

"Which almost never happens," Lord Artos squeaked. "Why, I don't remember the last time a Celestial unicorn came to visit Balinor! Not in my time, surely!"

Mr. Samlett, who had been helping Runetta clear the table, looked up as if he was about to speak. *He* had seen the Celestials. But at a warning glance from Ari, he said nothing.

"Celestial unicorns become mortal when they are here among us," Chase said. "If they do not return within a stated period of time to the Celestial Valley, they lose their immortality. And then they become prey to all the cares and sorrows of this world."

"You mean, they can be killed?" Lori asked.

64

"Oh, yes." Chase didn't move, but there was something sorrowful in the way he stood. Ari stroked his mane with gentle hands. "When any Balinor human or unicorn dies, we travel the Long Green Road into Summer. Summer is the gate to the worlds beyond. That is the last chance a Celestial has to return to the valley of its birth. Some are asked to rejoin the Celestial Valley herd. While others — others sleep in Summer. Forever."

Ari waited a moment while everyone thought about this. Then she got to her feet. "Now," she said, "we must plan. Chase and I will search for the lost Royal unicorns. Finn and Rednal will prepare the cavalry as the Royal unicorns come home. Runetta and Samlett? My faithful friends! You must prepare the members of the Resistance for a prolonged siege. We must be protected against all threats!"

Everyone murmured, "Hear! Hear!"

Ari placed her hands on the table and leaned forward earnestly. "Lord Puckenstew, I will leave you and the two other lords in charge of the army itself." She looked at each one of them in turn. "We have two weeks, my friends. Two weeks until the first night of the Shifter's Moon."

7

ight fell on the Valley of Fear. The half-
moon rode uneasily in the dull black sky. The slaves
in the Pit curled up to sleep after a meal of thin soup
and moldy bread. The soldiers of the Shifter's army
sat around campfires of damp coal, grumbling with
boredom and hate. No one had seen or heard from
the Shifter for a full day. Castle Entia brooded over
them all, a sullen beacon in the dark.

Lady Kylie slithered to the top of the tower
steps and pressed her ear against the wooden door.
Silence. She cocked her head and regarded the lock
with yellow slitted eyes. She would need hands for
this! She concentrated deeply. The Shifter allowed
her just enough of the shifting magic to transform
from a snake to a woman and back again. The easi-
est form to take was half-snake, half-human. She
chanted the shifting spell to herself. Her lipless
mouth vanished, and her hair curled black and

glossy around her shoulders. Her arms and hands formed easily out of her snaky skin. She resembled the person she had been before she had given herself heart and soul to the Shifter: the human Kylie, sister to Lord Lexan — the worst traitor in the history of Balinor.

She knocked at the door. No answer. "Master!" Kylie called. There was just the faintest hint of a hiss in her voice, but she sounded wholly human. "Entia?" Still no answer. She heard the hollow thump of iron hooves on stone. So he was in there, and in his unicorn form. "The troops are sitting idle. They want to know when we will attack!"

The door flew open with a sudden gust of wind. Kylie shrank back. Oily black smoke billowed from the room, blown about this way and that with the buffeting wind. Kylie shut her eyes against the storm and put her hands over her head. The wind died down as quickly as it had come. The quiet was eerie. Kylie peeked around the edge of the opened door.

Entia stood facing the wide window that opened out onto his domain. Smoke trailed from his muzzle. The room was a mess. Shards of broken glass were flung everywhere. The pedestal on which the Watching Bowl had stood lay broken in three pieces.

"Master?" Kylie poked tentatively through the mess. "No one has seen you, Great One!" she whined. "Your loyal subjects long for a glimpse of . . ."

The Shifter's hind feet kicked out. Kylie jumped away just in time. His right hind hoof whizzed past her face. He turned to her. His eyes glowed fiery red in his skull-like face. His iron horn burned red-hot. "I have a job for you," he grunted.

Kylie bowed so low that her chin brushed the floor. "Your wish is my command, master."

"Quiet! You are to be a spy in the palace."

Kylie straightened up, furious. "What! Me? They'll throw me in the dungeon!"

"SILENCE!" The Shifter's breath was flame. Kylie flung herself onto the floor again. "You will report back to me! You will tell me everything that Arianna is up to!"

Kylie waited until the flames were out. Then she said timidly, "But, Entia. Why not just repair the Watching Bowl?" She raised herself to her elbows. "It has helped us so much! I don't know why you didn't create it before!"

The Shifter's voice was a silky rumble of rage. "The watching magic is gone. *He* took it!"

"You mean . . ." Kylie looked fearfully around her. "Kraken. He is like that miserable Old Mare of the Mountain. Only on our side."

"There is no 'side' to the Deep Magic," the Shifter said. "It is all power. There is Shadow power and Celestial power. But it all comes from the same place." He didn't speak aloud the name of the One Who Rules. No one from the Shadow side ever did.

But that was where all magic came from — it was the source of the Deep Magic.

"I believe Kraken is on our side," Kylie said eagerly. "Does the Old Mare come to our aid when we are in need? We have never even seen the Old Mare! But Kraken! Look how he comes to help us."

"It is two faces of the same magic, you fool! For *them* — the face is that shaggy, spavined, sway-backed, thousand-year-old unicorn! For us . . ." He spat out the window. "The spider! It doesn't matter! Nothing matters but that I throw that bronze-haired brat and her arrogant unicorn into the deepest pit of the tower."

Kylie looked at the Shifter through half-closed eyes and wondered just how much magic the Shifter had left in him. For the brief time that Entia had held both the Indigo Star and the Royal Scepter, victory over Balinor and all the lands beyond had seemed assured. The Scepter and the Star were the most powerful talismans in the land. But he had lost the Scepter — and the Indigo Star, too. And now — Kylie mused to herself — now the Shifter's magic was the same as Princess Arianna's. Personal magic. Perhaps . . . she frowned uneasily. Perhaps even a bit less. Because the Princess had the Scepter to channel her magic. And the Shifter had nothing!

"Nothing? I have this!" he hissed. His iron horn glowed red-hot. Kylie cowered back.

"Oh, yes! I can read your mind! Never think

you can betray *me*, Kylie!" He advanced on her, his iron horn aimed straight at her heart. "My magic flows through my horn! You shall see it NOW!" In an instant, he transformed himself into a huge tiger, jaws dripping with poisonous slime. "And again!" he roared, and shifted into a toadlike beast with the fangs of a shark. "And again!" He shifted into a giant lizard, as tall as the ceiling, with claws of sharpened steel. His tongue darted out and stung Kylie's cheek. "I am the Shifter!" he whispered. "And the Royal magic doesn't — even — come — close!"

Kylie shrieked and scuttled away. The Shifter-lizard moved jerkily after her. Kylie felt like a fly, ready to be licked up and swallowed with one swipe of that terrible tongue.

The Shifter shoved his snout next to her ear. "Listen to me. I am going to tell you just once. You will disguise yourself. You will report back to me. And you will see that the high and mighty Sunchaser gets a little drop of this in his evening feed."

His mouth opened in a slow grin. Then he spat a small green pellet onto the floor. It rolled toward Kylie and stopped at the toe of her shoe.

"Pick it up!" the Shifter growled.

Kylie bent down and grabbed it. It stung her fingers. *Ah! Poison, then!* she thought as she slipped the pellet into the pouch at her belt.

"Now go!" the Shifter hissed. "And do not fail me! We have two weeks until we ride! Two weeks until the night of the Shifter's Moon!"

8

"It seems hard, milady, that you must prepare for a journey again. You just came home. It could be dangerous! What if you don't come home again?" Runetta wiped the tears from her cheeks. Then she added another warm pair of stockings to Ari's knapsack.

They were in the Royal mews, where Chase lived when he was at the palace, and Ari was in the middle of the preparations for her journey to find the Royal unicorns. She was glad Chase was back in his familiar stall, which was large and airy. The floor was clay, the most comfortable footing for unicorn hooves. Sweet oat straw lay in thick piles on the clay. Chase's cavalry harness and his parade saddle hung from polished pegs on the walls. The hay manger and feed buckets were of burnished bronze that glimmered in the twilight. Chase stood patiently with his head bent as Ari finished braiding his mane.

"I won't plague you anymore," Runetta said

stoutly. "Goodness knows you have enough to worry about without me crying all over you! What must be, must be."

"I'd give you a hug if I didn't need two hands to finish this braiding." Ari smoothed the last hairs into place.

"It looks so much nicer falling over his neck," Runetta said, briskly wiping the tears from her face. She was determined not to make Ari sad. "Why are you putting it into those little pigtails?"

Ari smiled. "This is the first time in a long while that I've had to really prepare for a journey, Runetta. One of the many reasons it's good to be home is that I have all of Chase's tack at hand." She brandished the silver mane pick. "It means I can fit Chase up to travel the way he should be! I know the braids in his mane aren't pretty, but they're neat. And he'll be much more comfortable without twigs getting in his hair."

"I'd be more comfortable with a thicker saddle pad," Chase chuckled. "Perhaps you could pack the one made of doubled wool, milady?"

"Of course, Chase. It's in the tack room at the other end of the mews. Come with me and we'll see how well it fits before I pack it."

Runetta smiled as she watched the Princess and her unicorn trot out the door to the back of the mews. While the Princess was gone, she could put a few more nourishing foods into the saddle-bag!

Runetta was so absorbed in her task that she jumped a foot when Lori bounced into the stall.

"Ari around?" she asked casually.

Runetta frowned at this form of address, then frowned even more at the person with Lori. "Her Royal Highness," she said, emphasizing the proper title, "will be back in a few moments. And who is this, Lady Lori?"

"This is Lady Kylian! Ari's new lady-in-waiting!" Lori said. "She just showed up a few minutes ago and applied for the job. I hired her. I thought she'd like to meet Ari before they left on this trip."

Runetta gasped. "You can't just hire a lady-in-waiting, my girl!"

Lori scowled horribly. "And why not?"

Runetta took a breath to tell Lori exactly why not.

"I am so grateful to be working for Her Royal Highness!" Lady Kylian sank to the floor of the stall in a deep bow. She was just as skinny as Lord Rexel. Her face was almost totally hidden by an elaborate headdress of pearls and satin.

That's her idea of the proper way for a lady-in-waiting to dress, Runetta supposed. Runetta nodded reluctantly. With all the terrible events going on around the palace, the last thing her Princess needed was another fuss! And the Princess could take care of this little problem after the bigger ones were solved. "We don't have much ceremony around the palace, Lady Kylian. You don't have to bow when we meet, for example." She held out her hand and Lady Kylian pulled herself upright and took it.

Runetta repressed a shudder. Lady Kylian's hand was dry and scaly.

"I'm anxious to begin serving Her Royal Highness."

Was that a lisp in Lady Kylian's speech? Runetta pushed away a faint unease. "I don't want you bothering Her Royal Highness right now, Lady Kylian! You go off with Lady Lori now! Maybe you can be of service while the Princess is gone. There's quite a bit for the ladies-in-waiting to do!"

"We have to buy clothes and jewels," Lori said.

"Nonsense!" Runetta briskly. "All of Princess Arianna's clothes must be aired, milady. And someone needs to see to cleaning up after those wicked soldiers! I told you how big a mess those kitchens are. Well, the palace is even worse! We'll have a proper spring cleaning while the Princess and His Majesty are gone!"

"I am *not* a maid," Lady Kylian rasped angrily. "I am an aristocrat!" She caught herself. All of a sudden, her voice became humble. "I mean, I am at Her Royal Highness's command." She crept forward and fingered Chase's saddlebags. "Stuffed full of grain!" she said. "Does Her Royal Highness make a long journey? Will there be a great deal to do before she and the Sunchaser return?"

Runetta closed the saddlebags against Lady Kylian's prying fingers. All of Arianna's most precious tools for magic were in them: the Royal Scepter, the Star Bottle from the Dreamspeaker, and the healing bag of little spells and charms Dr. Bohnes had given her when Ari and Chase had first returned home to Balinor. "Well!" Runetta said. "Thank you very much, Lady Lori. I am very happy to have Lady Kylian with us at the palace, and I'm sure the Princess will be, too. I'm sure if you take Lady Kylian to her rooms, Lori, I mean Lady Lori, you can get started on all those chores."

Lady Lori and Lady Kylian bowed themselves out of the stall. Runetta frowned when they were out of sight. "That's a fine one, and no mistake. I've never seen anyone less happy with a new job." But she broke into a smile as she heard the clop of the Sunchaser's hooves on the marble aisle. "There you are, milady! You just missed Lady Lori! She's hired a new lady-in-waiting, and there's something not quite right about her, but I'll make sure she works while you're gone!"

"Hired so quickly?" Ari said thoughtfully. She shook her head. "No matter. We must be off, Chase!"

"Do you know where to go, dear?" Runetta asked.

"East of the sun and west of the moon," Chase murmured.

"I'm sure I don't know what that means!"

Runetta shook her head and slipped another bag of apples into the food pack.

Ari gave Runetta a hug. "Having you here to help keeps me from missing Dr. Bohnes too much," she said.

Runetta blushed. "And how is she? I heard she wasn't well."

"We had a good talk before I left to come home," Ari said. "She'll recover, but slowly." There was a double door at the end of Chase's stall that led to a grassy paddock outside. It was open, and Ari could see the rising half-moon. *Two weeks*, she thought. *We have two weeks.* "She won't be well before we have to fight, Runetta. And I'm glad. I would worry about her in the middle of battle."

Runetta nodded. She folded her hands under her apron with a sigh. "Well, my dear! I believe you are packed."

"Yes," Ari said. "We're ready." She whistled and Lincoln came running in from the pasture he'd been inspecting. She cinched Chase's saddle, buckled the throat-latch on his bridle, then mounted with a quick spring. She and Chase trotted slowly into the dying light.

She looked back just once. Runetta waved good-bye. The warm lights of the mews barn shone around her. Finn and Rednal inspected a pile of old bridles and martingales. Rednal's snort of disgust floated across the cobbled yard; the Shifter's soldiers had left all the tack and harness in terrible disrepair.

She looked up at the palace. Lori waved from the second-floor balcony. She caught a glimpse of a woman in a hideous headdress standing next to Lori. It must be her new lady-in-waiting. She hoped they wouldn't quarrel!

Ari lifted her hand, then urged Chase forward. *Where should we go first, Chase?* she thought at him. *Where would you hide if you were hunted and stalked by our enemies?*

The Isle of the Unicorns, he replied. *We shall try there first. They would need water, grass, and a place to hide. The Isle of the Unicorns has all of those.*

The Isle of the Unicorns. Ari searched her memory. *That's east of here! A week's ride or more!*

As I said. East of the sun and west of the moon.

We must return in time, Chase! We must!

"Are you two talking to each other?" Linc said. He trotted briskly along. His white forepaws flashed a ghostly white. "Let me in on the conversation, will you?" He didn't wait for an answer, but bounded forward, his tail a happy plume. "I have a silent speech, too, you know! My nose!"

"Your nose?" Ari said.

"I can smell a Royal unicorn a mile away," the collie said confidently. "And I can track them, too. So if we can find the right general direction . . . I'll bring them all home!"

It took them six days to reach the spot where legend said the Isle of the Unicorns might be.

Chase's stride was long and he kept a steady pace. Ari had to resist the temptation to dawdle. She, Chase, and Lincoln were together, just the three of them! The weather was fine, with clear nights and warm days.

Ari felt guilty. She enjoyed being alone with her dog and her unicorn. They passed a village or two, but Ari had planned for a long journey, and there was no need to stop for extra food.

Toward the middle of the sixth day, the cultivated farmland turned to wilder country. Ari drew Chase to a halt and gazed around with pleasure. This part of Balinor was hilly, with groves of trees bunched attractively among rock-filled meadows and shallow valleys. There was a great deal of water; streams wandered into tiny lakes, tiny lakes into bigger ones. Small waterfalls splashed happily under the wide blue sky. "I don't believe I've ever been into this part of Balinor, Chase."

Lincoln yawned and stretched. "I vote we take a break."

"We really shouldn't," Ari said regretfully. "What do you think, Chase?"

"We've gone east of the sun. It's now time to go west of the moon." The giant bronze unicorn stood with his muzzle to the breeze. "I'm not precisely sure where that is," he admitted after a moment. "We may have to ask the way from here."

"Let's ask that guy in the boat," Lincoln said.

He stood with his ears tuliped forward. His plumy tail waved gently.

"What boat?" Ari shaded her eyes with her hands. They were directly in front of a miniature lake, and sure enough, a small red boat sailed on the sparkling water.

"It's an old guy wearing a hat," Lincoln said, although by now Ari could see that for herself. The boat tacked back and forth, heading in to shore. Ari tapped Chase with her heels, and he waded hock-high into the water. Lincoln waded after them, sniffing eagerly. "Fish!" he barked happily. "He's got a load of fish!"

The sailor waved casually at them. He was small, with a thick chest and heavily muscled forearms. He had a short white beard and merry blue eyes. Ari waved back. There was a name printed in white on the hull, and Ari caught her breath in excitement. "Chase! Do you see the name on the boat?"

"I do indeed, milady. It seems we have come to the right place."

"Well?" Lincoln after a moment.

"Well what?" Ari looked at him.

"What's the name on the boat?"

"You can see for yourself, Linc."

"Dogs can't read!"

"Oh." Ari bit her lip. "Sorry. Her name is *Moon*."

"East of the sun and west of the . . . oh! We *have* come to the right place!" Lincoln grinned happily. The question about Lincoln that Ari had set aside for so long because of all her adventures returned to her again. Who *was* Lincoln? She had never seen any collies other than her own in Balinor. On the other side of the Gap — where she had been hidden by the loyal members of the Resistance — there were plenty of collies. If, like Lori, Lincoln belonged to the world of Glacier River, should he eventually return there?

"He has fish!" Linc said happily. "I can smell them! I love roasted fish!"

The *Moon* bumped the shoreline. Ari brought herself out of her thoughts with a jerk. "Ahoy, there!" the sailor called. "Grab on to that line there, missy!" He threw a rope from the bow and Ari caught it midair. She slid off Chase into the water, waded to shore, and fixed the line firmly around a tree stump.

The sailor jumped out handily and waded toward her, hand extended into welcome. "Avast there, missy! Cap'n Betlett at your service!"

Ari shook his rough, callused hand. He promptly sat down, removed his boots, and poured the water out. His shrewd blue eyes looked Ari up and down. "Looks like you're far from home, missy," he offered.

"My name is Ari. This is Chase and this is Lincoln."

80

"Fine dog there." He nodded. "And an even finer unicorn!"

"Thank you," Chase said gravely. "We are in need of some assistance, Captain Betlett. I am looking for my herdmates."

"Ah," the captain said.

"Unicorns," Ari supplied. "About thirty of them."

"Oh?"

"They — um." Ari hesitated. This cheerful person couldn't possibly be on the side of the Shifter! But she couldn't trust anyone nowadays. Not with so much at stake. "We've lost them, so to speak."

The captain eyed her for a long, long minute. "But the question is, missy: Do they want to be found?"

9

Captain Betlett was as suspicious of Ari and Chase as they were of him, and so it took a lot of talking before they got down to the business of finding the lost unicorns. At Lincoln's wistful look, Ari asked if she could purchase part of the captain's catch, and after a bit of haggling, they settled on a price. "And," the captain said, pocketing the coins Ari gave him, "seeing as how we agreed on a fine price for the fish, well, I'll just roast a few of them right here for you, missy!"

Lincoln was a great help in collecting a pile of branches for a fire, and soon the three of them were sitting around the flames, roasting the fish on sticks. Chase, with an amused shake of his head, grazed on the short, sweet grass.

"So you're looking for unicorns!" the captain asked after they had eaten their fill. "Lots of fine ones in the village of Kapnor a few miles back." His shrewd blue eyes traveled over Chase's bronze coat. The sun was sinking into the west, and it shone with more than its usual brightness. "But they don't look like him. Is it specific unicorns? Or just unicorns in general that you seek?"

Ari decided to take a chance. "Ones that I've known and loved," she said slowly. "There's Tierza. She's glossy black, with a sweet face and a mane as soft as a spiderweb. She has a jewel at the base of her horn, Captain Betlett. The jewel is as blue as her eyes. And Flier. Well, that's his stable name. He's registered as Fly Away Home, and he is as brown as a mink and just as glowing. His jewel is clear amber and so is his horn. And Beecher! How could I forget Beecher! She's a gray with a milk-white horn and tail. Her trot is as long and graceful as that gull flying over the lake."

Captain Betlett took a smelly pipe from his waistcoat pocket and knocked it on the ground. Then he stuffed it full of tobacco and stuck it in his mouth. But he didn't light the pipe, and he grinned at Ari's inquiring expression. "Mrs. Cap'n," he said, by way of explanation. "Made me quit, you see. But I still like to hold it once in a while. Now then, missy. You seem to know these unicorns. Knowledge that only someone from, say, the Royal Palace might have. Now, you wouldn't be forgetting a unicorn two shades darker than a gold coin, with a cream-colored horn and a mane and tail to match?"

"Sunburst!" Ari said. "Of course I haven't forgotten Sunburst!"

"Or a nice spotted one, red and black and white? With a red horn, black mane, and white tail."

"Puzzler!" Ari shouted. "You know where they are!"

"Maybe I do and maybe I don't." Captain Betlett sucked on his cold pipe. "Question *I* have is, how do *you* know who they are? Now, you have the look of a girl who knows her unicorns." He tapped her knee with the pipe. "You maybe work somewhere special?" He winked. "Like —" He leaned forward and whispered in her ear. (His breath was quite fishy.) "The Royal mews?"

Ari whispered back, "Yes! I've worked in the Royal mews!" Which was perfectly true, because she didn't allow anyone else to care for Chase except herself.

"Ah! Thing is, these are dark days. And you don't know who might be after them — the Royals, I mean. Until His Majesty, bless him, returns to the throne, you don't know who to trust. Now, they say —"

"Who says?" Ari asked, curious, because people were always saying "they say" and she wanted to know where the captain's information was coming from. "Who is 'they'?"

"The villagers, where I go to trade my fish. They say the young Princess is back. Her Royal Highness, Princess Arianna." He sighed. "If I should

84

live to see that day! I saw her once, when she was just a little 'un, before she went through the bonding with His Majesty, the Sunchaser. Beautiful little thing. Big eyes like sapphires. Hair like molten bronze. She bid to be as fair as her lady-mother, the Queen, bless them both." His eyes narrowed. "You said your name is Ari? Why, you aren't Princess Arianna, are you?"

"Well, I . . ."

He sighed, a looming deep sigh. "I see." He bowed before Ari. "Then I'll take you to them. All of you."

And with the sun setting over the lake they set sail in the *Moon*. Ari enjoyed the peace and calm of the water. The breeze had died down a bit, and they slid over the ripples with no noise but the flapping of the mainsail and soft jingle of the lines on the jib. They sailed east of the setting sun, and when the quarter-moon rose, Captain Betlett tacked west. Ari's heart sank at the sight of the fading Silver Traveler.

The time was speeding by so fast!

As the sun sent the last peach ray over the softly swelling hills, the captain pointed into the mist rising from the water. "There," he said. "The Isle of the Unicorns."

It was a small island, thick with trees around the outer rim. With the last of the sun, the breeze quieted entirely. Ari helped the captain set sail — not an easy task in a small boat carrying a large dog and an even larger unicorn. The captain took a long set of oars from the bulwarks and rowed them into shore.

They landed with a soft bump. For a moment, Ari didn't hear anything except the gentle splash of the waves against the hull. Then the tree frogs resumed their peeping. A night bird called out and flew up into the moonlight. There was a rustle in the brush and an angry voice called out, "Who goes there!"

"It's the cap'n!" He winked at Ari. "I bring oats over to them on a reg'lar basis, like." He raised his voice. "I got some friends you might want to see!"

A long horn poked through the bushes. In the twilight, Ari could just make out the color. Red. It was Puzzler! "Who are these friends, Betlett?" Puzzler demanded. "You know who searches for us! And they are no friends of ours!"

"Wait!" Chase called out. "You know my voice as well as you know me! But beware, my friend! No names! Not in the dark of this night!"

"Ch —" Puzzler bit Chase's name off just in time. "Your Maj . . . I . . ." He stopped himself again. "Is it really you?"

"Of course it is," Chase said reassuringly. "You will let us land, herdmate? No charges out of the bush, if you please!"

"You're asking *my* permission, Your Maj — I mean Sun — I mean, yes!"

Heart pounding with excitement, Ari scrambled out of the *Moon* and onto dry land. Lincoln sprang beside her. Chuckling, Captain Betlett anchored the line to a large stone.

They all pushed into the brush after Chase. The thick circle of trees and brush surrounding the Isle of the Unicorn was better protection than a stone wall. Ari could hardly squeeze herself through. The unicorns had their horns, but Chase, concerned for Ari's safety, circled back and began to forge a path with his hooves and horn. His efforts didn't help much since the branches flew back in her face as fast as Chase bent them aside. But she forged on. She saw flashes of bronze (Chase), cream and mahogany (Linc), and more leaves and branches than she ever wanted to see again in her whole life.

She finally broke through to a clearing right in the center of the island. The quarter-moon was weak and cast a pale light over the scene. A herd of unicorns clustered on the grass. The jewels at the base of their horns flashed subdued colors in the dim light. It looked as though multicolored fireflies danced around the grove.

They had found the Royal unicorns!

10

"Tierza! Flier! Beecher!" As Ari called their names, each unicorn ran forward and bowed gracefully at her feet. Tears of joy ran down Ari's cheeks. They were all here! All of them! Safe from the Shifter's evil! She ran her hands over their faces and kissed each soft muzzle. They shouted with joy as they greeted Ari and Chase. They plunged around the clearing, kicking their heels to the sky, then whirling and rearing high.

Captain Betlett leaned against a tree, arms folded, his unlit pipe in his mouth. Lincoln sat near him, prudently out of the way of the excited unicorns. The collie glanced up at the honest fisherman: The captain was getting a little teary, too! "Do you come here often, Captain Betlett?"

"Oh, aye. Once a month, sometimes more often. The Royals have a lot of good grass here, and there's a stream over yonder for water. But these unicorns are too hot-blooded to do well on grass alone. They need oats. So I bring what I can, when I can."

Ari, settling down at last, had noticed that many of the taller Royals were ribby. She went to Chase, who was standing with Puzzler. "Some of the unicorns are too thin, Chase," she said worriedly. "And others look just fine. You haven't had enough to eat, Puzzler, I can tell from the way your withers stick out. But Tierza looks healthy." The beautiful black unicorn was chatting happily to Lincoln. Her sides were round and sleek.

The big, spotted unicorn shifted in an embarrassed way. "Captain Betlett has been a good friend to us," he said. "He brings oats as often as he can. But the smaller unicorns need more food than we do." Ari knew this wasn't true — the bigger unicorns needed more food. "So they get first pick of the oats."

Ari took a moment to look all the unicorns over carefully. "What's happened here is that you've given the fillies and the mares the oats, Puzzler," she scolded gently. "But the captain has more oats in the boat."

"And I have my portion as well," Chase said. "We will bring the oats out and eat before we begin the journey home. And perhaps we can stop in the village near here to get some more."

"You have oats?" Puzzler said with a hopeful gleam in his eye. "Enough for all?"

"Enough for all!" Ari said. And in a few minutes, they had unloaded the bag of oats from the *Moon*. Ari portioned them out equally to all. But Puzzler insisted on waiting until all the others had been fed, and by the time Ari got to him the sack was empty. She reached into Chase's saddlebag. There were four feeds in the bag, enough to sustain Chase on the journey back to the palace.

Give him as much as he wants, Chase said to her in their silent speech. *The poor fellow has been hungry for too long!*

Ari just smiled. She loved Chase, but she knew him (and all other unicorns!) too well to agree to give Puzzler as many oats as he could eat. Unicorns loved oats, and, indeed, grains of all kinds. If their riders weren't careful with feed portions, a unicorn would eat until he colicked! She opened the saddle-bag and scooped two measures of oats in front of Puzzler; then she offered some to Chase, who shook his head. "He'll need more later, milady," he said in an undertone. "I can skip a few meals."

"Thank you, Your Royal Highness!" Puzzler bent eagerly to the oats.

"Wait!" Ari said. "There's something round in there, Puzzler. Let me check the grain."

But the big unicorn gulped the full portion of oats before she could move.

At first, everything seemed fine. Puzzler licked the grass clean of all the oats and heaved a big sigh of relief. "That was delicious!" he said politely. "Except for that little bitter piece in the middle, Chase. Are you taking some kind of . . ." He stopped in midspeech, an odd expression on his face. "Some kind of . . ." He took a deep breath. Then another. His sides began to heave in and out with great gasping breaths. Sweat poured down his withers and patched his chest.

"He's colicking," Ari said worriedly. "He must have eaten too quickly. Whoa, Puzzler. Whoa." She put a gentling hand on his neck. Her hand was drenched with his sweat.

Puzzler fell to the ground with a huge thump. The other Royals gathered around him in a worried circle. His legs thrashed. His breathing became shallower and shallower. Ari knelt by his head. With one hand, she fumbled in the saddlebags, searching for Dr. Bohnes's bag of healing potions. The potions had saved them all once before in the Valley of Fear. They had to save Puzzler now!

Chase stood like a statue, his eyes fixed on his herdmate's agonized face. Ari shook the contents of Dr. Bohnes's bag onto the ground. A glass bottle rolled free of the spilled contents. She grabbed it and peered at the label in the weak moonlight.

The label said REMEDY (DO NOT USE IN CONJUNCTION WITH OTHER MAGIC).

Puzzler's eyes rolled back in his head. His muzzle opened wide. He tried to take a breath, but the spasms in his stomach were so severe, he couldn't. His eyes glazed. A weird green color crept behind the pupils.

"The Long Green Road!" Tierza cried. "He sets a foot on the Long Green Road!"

"No!" Ari cried. The Scepter! She had to use the Scepter! What if the remedy didn't work? And if it didn't work, she couldn't use the Scepter, because the Scepter was magic. But this wasn't magic. She knew what this was. Poison! Someone had put poison in Chase's food!

And if she used the Scepter, the Shifter would find them! And the Royals were too weak from lack of good food to fight well.

Ari closed her eyes. She would call on Atalanta. The Dreamspeaker would advise her!

"Milady?" Chase's voice was calm, but Ari could hear undercurrents of terror for his friend. "He will walk the Long Green Road if we do not save him."

She couldn't risk it. She couldn't risk them all for the sake of the one. Ari grabbed the bottle and forced the contents down poor Puzzler's throat. He gasped. Then choked. His breathing stilled. His eyes closed. Nearby, Lincoln sent a lonely howl skyward. Ari bit her lip to keep from crying aloud. She was their leader. She couldn't break down now. "Oh, Dreamspeaker," she said softly. "Please save this good unicorn." She laid her hands on either side of Puzzler's head. She bent over him, her hair falling all around his muzzle.

She felt a faint breath on her cheek.

Then another.

And then Puzzler began to breathe normally.

Ari fell back onto the grass in relief. She stared up at the sky while the Royal unicorns milled excitedly around Puzzler. Lincoln came and curled next to her side. "Are you okay?" he asked worriedly.

"I think so." Ari sat up abruptly. "All I can think of is — what if it hadn't worked?"

"The potion?" Lincoln nudged her with his nose. She scratched absentmindedly behind his ears. "Do you think Lori would want to be the Princess for a while?" she asked after a long moment. "Or maybe Lord Puckenstew would like to be King."

"You're asking me?" The collie sat up and looked at her gravely.

"I know what Chase would say," Ari replied ruefully. "He would sympathize and comfort me, and then tell me we have to go on. I don't think I can go on, Linc. I'm a terrible Princess. What if I had killed Puzzler? What if the potion hadn't worked? I should have used the Scepter," she muttered. "I couldn't have borne it if that poor unicorn had walked the Long Green Road."

"Many more would have died if the Shifter discovered us before we were ready to fight," Lincoln said. "There are no easy decisions, Ari."

Ari stroked his ears and thought longingly of Glacier River Farm. She had been a mere stable girl there. She had no terrible responsibilities. No one's life was in her hands. "I could use the Scepter to get through the Gap," she said in a whisper. "Don't you want to go home, Linc?"

"Home," the collie said wistfully. "My home is where you are, Ari."

"And my home," Ari said slowly, "my home is with them." She felt Chase's warm, loving gaze on her. Puzzler was standing up. The ominous green glow in his eyes was gone. So he would not travel the Long Green Road into Summer this night — and, Ari hoped, not for many years to come.

"Your Royal Highness!" Tierza shouted. "We need you here!"

Slowly, Ari got to her feet. Somehow, the Shifter had put poison into Chase's feed. They would have to be careful all the way back to the palace. Enemies were all around them!

She dusted herself off and went to help her unicorns. They would all march home. And then the battle against the Shifter would begin.

11

❧

"**W**hat if Lady Kylian is right?" Lori asked Finn nervously. "What if the Shifter has a secret weapon to use against us?" She stood first on one foot, then the other. She and Finn were outside the Royal mews, ready to go into the palace for dinner. Ari and Chase had been gone for almost two weeks. And there had been no word of their whereabouts.

"What kind of a secret weapon would it be?" Finn asked in a sensible tone. "And why would Kylian know about it and no one else? I have to tell you, Lori. I don't like that woman one bit. I don't think you should have hired her — not without checking with Her Royal Highness first."

Lori had been having doubts about Lady Kylian, too. But she wasn't about to admit it to Finn. "In this crazy place, a secret weapon could be anything!" Lori said.

"What crazy place?"

"Balinor," Lori said.

Finn rolled his eyes. "I forgot. You're not from around here. Well, what makes this place crazier than any other place?"

"There aren't any cars, for one thing," Lori said. "And no malls, if you can believe that. And there's no CDs, no eyeliner or mascara —"

"I don't know what any of those things are, and I don't want to know," Finn said in a this-is-the-end-of-this-discussion tone of voice.

"And there's the magic. I've never been any-place where there's magic." She adjusted her head-dress firmly. It was quite a nice headdress, woven of gold mesh with pearls twined all around it.

Finn decided to try to change the subject. "That's a new headdress, isn't it?"

Lori's sullen expression brightened. "Kylian bought it for me. Well, she didn't buy it exactly, be-cause Ari left without leaving me a dress allowance like she promised. But I told the jeweler that he could be the Royal jeweler when Ari got back, so he said he'd wait to get paid."

"Do you think you should have done that?"

Lori tossed her head. "And why not?"

Finn just sighed. Lori had three new dresses of expensive silk and brocade, too. Ari would just have to deal with it when she got back. *If* she got back. He looked up anxiously at the sky. The sun was setting and the last sliver of the moon hung pale and wan in the sky. Tomorrow night would be the first night of the Shifter's Moon. The night when there was no moon.

The night when the battle was foretold to begin.

They left the mews and began to walk to the palace. Finn glanced over his shoulder to make sure all was in order. It was quite a task, being captain of the Royal cavalry, and he took his duties seriously. Rednal and Toby were safe and snug in their stalls, eating their evening ration of oats. A few Worker unicorns from the village had arrived at the mews over the past few days and volunteered to join the cavalry. Finn had been busy schooling them in war maneuvers. Rednal was a great help, showing the others how to lean and spin so that the enemy couldn't spear them with their horns. And Toby had been exceptional at demonstrating various kicks and high jumps.

Finn ran up the broad palace steps, leaving Lori to trail behind.

"There you are, young Master!" Runetta beamed. "Just in time for the evening meal!"

Finn approached the Great Hall and stood outside the door, hesitating. The Lords of Balinor had called all their knights-at-arms to gather and help in the coming war, and the room was filled with them. Lord Puckenstew's knights were built just like him — big and hairy. Lord Artos's knights were taller than everyone else, as if the very short lord were trying to make up for his own lack of height.

And Lord Rexel's knights were skinny and gaunt because Rexel was so cheap and didn't feed them properly, which didn't surprise anyone. Runetta made sure they all got lots of food.

Finn took a place at the end of the table farthest from the pyramid of thrones, which happened to be where Rexel and Lady Kylian were sitting. Samlett had scoured the palace basements for tables to accommodate the extra people. The Great Hall was jam-packed with townspeople, knights, fishermen from Sixton, even the Dragonslayers who had helped Ari and Chase when the dragon Naytin had been on the prowl.

"Cavalry ready to fight?" Lord Rexel stuffed a piece of bread into his mouth and observed Finn narrowly. "How many unicorns and riders do you have, boy?"

"Ssssurely . . . I mean," Lady Kylian corrected herself. "Surely you don't have too many?"

Finn wished he could see under the elaborate headdress Kylian always wore. He hadn't liked her much when she'd appeared at the palace the day Ari and Chase left, and he liked her even less as time went on. He thought there was something reptilian about her. And he wasn't about to tell her anything about the cavalry.

"Six!" Lori said, plumping herself down next to Finn. She reached over and grabbed the last slice of bellymelon, a fruit that Finn especially liked. "And out of that six, one is a Draft unicorn about a hundred years old, and another's got splints . . ."

"S-s-splints?" Lady Kylian asked.

"You know, where the tendons in the leg get all puffy." Lori swallowed her bellymelon with a gulp. "Happens to horses, too."

"Horses?" Lord Rexel wiped his mouth with his sleeve and slouched back in his chair. "What are horses?"

"Never mind," Lori muttered. "You people don't know anything!" She glanced at Finn. "Finn's done a good job with what he's got, though."

"It will not be enough!" Lady Kylian shook her head back and forth. She swayed in her chair. Finn watched her, fascinated. "It will not be enough against the forces of the Shifter!"

"We'll see," Finn said easily. "Her Royal Highness will be back any day now. And then the Royal unicorns will join us. They are mighty fighters. Rednal says so."

"Ah. But will she be back? And will the Sunchaser be with her?" The last rays of the sun slipped away as Kylian spoke and the room fell into twilight. Samlett and Runetta busied themselves lighting the torches.

"Many things can happen on such a perilous journey," Kylian said.

"The moon's almost out," Lori said. "Look! You can barely see it!"

"Then *he* will come." The headdress slipped away from Kylian's face as she spoke. Finn shuddered. Her whole face was caked with powder. She looked like a ghost sitting there. "And he will have a weapon with Shadow magic in it."

All around them, people had stopped eating and chattering to listen. "What is this weapon?" Finn said loudly. "I don't believe in it."

"Nor I!" said a stout knight in the pale blue of Puckenstew's House. "What kind of lady-in-waiting are you? You're just trying to scare us!"

Suddenly, all the torches in the Great Hall went out, as if doused by a giant fist. A great wind rose and blew through the hall, sweeping platters and trenchers from the tables and whipping cloaks, surcoats, and jerkins off the people sitting there. The wind screamed around the hall and pulled Kylian's headdress from her face. Lori jumped to her feet and pointed. She screamed and screamed again: "IT'S HER! IT'S HER! IT'S THE SNAKEWOMAN!"

Finn drew his short sword and jumped over the table. Kylie's evil face twisted with horrible laughter. She slipped away from Finn and writhed on the floor.

"She's turning into a snake!" someone shouted, and the entire hall broke into shouts of terror.

"He comessss!" Kylie shouted gleefully. "My massssster comes!"

Finn ran to the huge window overlooking Balinor Village. Thunderclouds rose out of the west, obscuring the thin moon. Lightning forked through the darkened skies. The wind whirled wildly through the village, overturning carts, pulling off roofs, a mad tornado of destruction.

And from the west, the home of the Shifter, a huge blackness came, a giant winged bat with red eyes. Below it raced a battalion of Shadow unicorns, ridden by skeletal soldiers.

"Close the gates!" Finn shouted. He raced out of the palace to the moat, his heart pounding. "CLOSE THE GATES!"

War had begun!

12

"Storm's coming," Lincoln said, his nose quivering.

Ari reined Chase in at the top of a small rise. They were a half hour away from home. The Royal unicorns fanned out behind them like a gorgeous train on a ball gown. Everyone was weary from the long trek. They had galloped long and hard, fearful of what was happening at home. Ari wanted nothing more than a hot bran mash for Chase and a hot bath for herself. She looked anxiously at Lincoln. The sun had set just a moment ago, and the sky was dull with the lack of moonlight. "What kind of a storm?" She remembered the flight of Naytin the dragon and how horrific the dragon storm had been.

Linc flattened his ears and sniffed the breeze. "Not natural," he said. "There's no rain coming. And it's not the dragon." But his tone was not at all reassuring.

Chase moved uneasily beneath her. Puzzler galloped up to them. The whites of his eyes were showing. "Something's wrong," he said abruptly. "The air feels wrong." Lightning streaked on the western horizon.

Chase whirled on his hindquarters and faced directly west. He said tensely, "Look!"

A great shadow loomed out of the west. Giant wings formed. Hot red eyes glared down at Balinor. Ari's breath failed her. She knew those eyes! "The Shifter," she said quietly. "Too soon. Too soon."

"But how?" Lincoln burst out. "We thought we had more time!"

"Don't you see, Lincoln?" Chase bent his great head to look directly at the collie. "The poison in the feed. That was meant for me. And you know who put it there."

"The Shifter," Ari said in the same quiet tone. "Somehow!" She turned in the saddle. Her gaze swept over the herd of Royal unicorns. "The Shifter has come!" There was no panic in her voice, only resolve. "We must ride to the palace! We must ride for life and for Balinor!" She drew the Royal Scepter from the saddlebag where she had kept it carefully wrapped these two long weeks. She held it up. "Give me light!" she said, and the Scepter sprang into vivid brilliance. The white light spread around Ari and Chase like a great veil. "Throw your hearts over, my friends! Stop for nothing! And follow the Sunchaser!"

103

She had no need to cue Chase. He leaped into a hand gallop. She raised herself out of the saddle and bent low over his neck, barely aware of the thundering herd behind her. She kept a sharp eye on the ground for holes, for traps for Chase's hooves. He leaped over fences and ditches, Puzzler and Tierza hot behind him. Lincoln barked and barked again. He was falling behind, no match for the long legs and incredible speed of the racing Royals.

The miles flashed by. Above them, the Shifter's storm thundered and crashed. They galloped through the village, where they had marched in triumph three weeks before. They swept past the fork in the road and galloped up the hill to the palace.

At the very top, Ari drew rein and looked upon the battle. Chase danced angrily. She drew him firmly in.

"Let me go!" he shouted. For the first time in his life, he fought her, shaking his head angrily against the restraining reins. He reared, his forelegs pawing the sky.

Below them, the Shifter's army swarmed over the palace gates. Behind them, the Royals surged like an angry sea. Above them, the Shifter hovered, a giant bat-form.

"HOLD!" Ari shouted. "HOLD ON!"

Chase quieted, trembling. His withers ran with sweat.

Ari's gaze swept the battleground. Rednal

and Finn were at the head of a pitifully small group of cavalry at the drawbridge. Rednal reared and turned, his horn a deadly weapon. Finn's sword cut through the attacking Shadow unicorns and their riders.

But the enemy's numbers were overwhelming.

The knights from the great Houses of Balinor stood on the palace walls, knocking off the Shifter's soldiers as they scaled the stone.

But there were too many! There were hundreds of them!

"We only have thirty Royals," Ari said to Chase calmly. "Thirty horns to attack so many. It won't work."

"We have to try, milady!" He struggled against the restraining reins again. "Let me go!"

"If we attack from here, we will all die," Ari said. She raised her eyes to the sky. The Shifter swooped and flew. She heard a faint and terrible laughter.

Ari transferred the reins to the hand that held the Scepter, and then fumbled in the saddlebags over Chase's flanks. The veil! She had to have the veil! She drew it out and flung it skyward. It settled over her shoulders, over Chase's hindquarters, blooming rosy red with a terrible beauty.

"Atalanta!" Ari said. "It is time!" She closed her eyes. She put all her will, all her knowledge of herself and her people, into a fierce burst of energy and desire. Her will flowed through her, through Chase, and into the Scepter.

The white light exploded silently, like a huge silver sun. A single broad ray reached to the sky.

"Atalanta!" Ari shouted. "For my mother! My father! My brothers! And for Balinor!"

The ray of light coalesced and solidified into an arch. It hung from the sky to the earth, a pure white path. The Shifter flew above it, below it, with angry screams.

The sky opened.

The Celestials marched down the bridge of light. Atalanta and Numinor were at the head of the Rainbow herd. Atalanta's violet eyes were fierce. She wore a breastplate of hammered silver, and her flanks were covered with silver shields. Numinor, beside her, was arrayed in gold. And all of the unicorns behind them shone with their own band of rainbow color.

Midway down the path of light, the Shifter flew at the Dreamspeaker. Numinor gave a battle cry, a huge bellow that shook the world with the sound of a great gold hammer. He leaped, used his horn as a spear, and plunged it into the Shifter's dark heart.

The Shifter screamed, a long wailing cry that stilled the attack of the Shadow unicorns. Everyone looked skyward. The arch of light broadened until it formed a vast plain. The Rainbow herd overwhelmed the bat shape. Each time their horns plunged into the rotten dark shape, the bat shrank, until finally there was nothing left to spear.

The sky cleared, but the arch of light held fast. The glorious Celestials formed the Rainbow and the victorious arch lit up the scene with a flood of color. Atalanta turned. She looked down on Ari and the Sunchaser. Her great eyes glowed. She nodded.

It is up to you now, Arianna!

Ari nodded.

Atalanta faced the gate that Ari had opened for her. She walked back up the path of light. The Celestials followed her, one by one.

The rainbow faded.

For a moment, all on the battlefield were silent. The Shifter was gone. Ari replaced the Scepter in her saddlebag and gave her orders. "Chase and I will ride to the aid of Finn and Rednal. Puzzler, take fifteen Royals to the south wall. Tierza, take the others to the north wall. Take prisoners, if you can. If the enemy runs off, do not follow. We must retake the palace first."

"Well, I knew there was something wrong with that Lady Kylian from the very first," Lori said. They were all sitting around a warm fire in the Great Hall. The Royal unicorns had made short work of what was left of the Shifter's army. Most of the soldiers and Shadow unicorns had run off after the defeat of their master. But a few had been captured.

Ari had given orders to lock them up in the very unpleasant dungeons in the palace grounds. She would turn them over to the townspeople for trial, after they'd been fed and their wounds attended to.

Finn gave Ari a rueful smile. "We should have suspected something from the very first!"

"Thank goodness it turned out all right," Runetta said.

"Yes," Ari said. "I hope that we will never see the likes of the Shifter again."

"And I missed seeing the Dreamspeaker again," Lincoln said sadly. "We dogs just can't run as fast as unicorns. By the time I reached the palace, the battle was won!"

"This time," Chase said. He dropped his muzzle into Ari's shoulder and breathed lightly. "You were right to restrain me, milady. If we had raced to the attack, we would have been overwhelmed."

Ari patted his nose. "It all turned out for the best, didn't it?"

"So everything's okay?" Lori asked. "We're all safe, and you can be the Princess again? Because . . . um . . . about these bills I have for all the dresses I needed for being your lady-in-waiting . . ."

Ari grinned and stretched her feet toward the fire. Chase was at her side. Lincoln was at her feet. But the battles were *never* over!

In the Valley of Fear, the fires leaped high in the desert and then went out. The chains on the prisoners in the Pit burst with a shrill metallic clang. The slaves scrambled up the sides of the Pit to freedom.

A terrible rumbling shook the earth. The towers of Castle Entia shook with the fearsome quake. The highest tower, Entia's tower, swayed back and forth in the glowering dark, then toppled to the ground with a roar.

The Valley of Fear was destroyed.

For a long while, nothing moved in the desert. Then the wind picked up, hot and chill by turns, although no being was there to feel it.

The wind died. The Pit yawned empty in the all but moonless night. Then a crack appeared at the bottom. A skeletal hand emerged, and the rest of a dark and shadowy figure crawled out and up the stony stairs.

The wind picked up. If any had been around to hear, the voices in the wind would have frozen them in terror. "Kraken!" the voices hissed. "Kraken will rebuild!"

About the Author

Mary Stanton loves adventure. She has lived in Japan, Hawaii, and all over the United States. She has held many different jobs, including singing in a nightclub, working for an advertising agency, and writing for a TV cartoon series. Mary lives on a farm in upstate New York with some of the horses who inspire her to write adventure stories like the UNICORNS OF BALINOR.

Rockett's World ™

GET READY!
GET SET!
READ ROCKETT!

$3.99 each

Meet the Guardians of the Force.

JEDI APPRENTICE

$4.99 Each!

☐ BDN51922-0 **#1: The Rising Force**

☐ BDN51925-5 **#2: The Dark Rival**

☐ BDN51933-6 **#3: The Hidden Past**

☐ BDN51934-4 **#4: The Mark of the Crown**